Ellie was changed when she came out of the coma.

Not that I expected the exact same flaky, sixteen-year-old we'd all known and loved, not after she'd been dead to the world so long. The doctors warned me that some cognitive changes were inevitable.

But this was something else. This was someone else.

She awoke looking just like her sixteen-year-old self–the same straight black hair, the same round face and pale skin. But she wasn't really Ellie. Not anymore.

Someone else looked out through her owlish blue eyes.

I'd been with her every day. I'd even brought Blanky–yes, that's what she still called the ratty old blanket she'd kept since childhood and slept with every night, even as a teen–and I kept it by her side.

And then in early May she came to. Like someone awakening from a nap, she opened her eyes and said, "I want to go home."

No disorientation, no asking what had happened. It seemed as if she'd been aware all along.

As I looked at her I felt my initial burst of joy wither in the cold certainty that Ellie wasn't back. Not really. Not my Ellie.

As I was hustled out of the unit by the nurses flocking around her, I heard her voice rise about the hubbub: "Mother? Mother, did you hear me? I want to go home!"

Ellie has never called me "Mother." Never.

I stood in the doorway, staring back at my younger daughter, and thinking this has to be strangest moment of my life. But I was wrong. So, so wrong. Things hadn't begun to get strange.

SIGNALZ

An Adversary Cycle Novel

(Prelude to *Nightworld*)

F. PAUL WILSON

OTHER BOOKS BY F. PAUL WILSON

Repairman Jack*

The Tomb	Harbingers
Legacies	Bloodline
Conspiracies	By the Sword
All the Rage	Ground Zero
Hosts	The Last Christmas
The Haunted Air	Fatal Error
Gateways	The Dark at the End
Crisscross	Nightworld
Infernal	Quick Fixes—Tales of Repairman Jack

The Teen Trilogy*

Jack: Secret Histories
Jack: Secret Circles
Jack: Secret Vengeance

The Early Years Trilogy*

Cold City
Dark City
Fear City

The Adversary Cycle*

The Keep	Reborn
The Tomb	Reprisal
The Touch	Nightworld

Omnibus Editions

The Complete LaNague
Calling Dr. Death (3 medical thrillers)
Ephemerata

Novellas

*The Peabody-Ozymandias Traveling Circus & Oddity Emporium**
*"Wardenclyffe"**
*"Signalz"**

The LaNague Federation

Healer
Wheels Within Wheels
An Enemy of the State
Dydeetown World
The Tery

Other Novels

*Black Wind**	*Deep as the Marrow*
*Sibs**	*Sims*
The Select	*The Fifth Harmonic**
Virgin	*Midnight Mass*
Implant	

Collaborations

Mirage (with Matthew J. Costello)
Nightkill (with Steven Spruill)
Masque (with Matthew J. Costello)
Draculas (with Crouch, Killborn, Strand)
The Proteus Cure (with Tracy L. Carbone)
A Necessary End (with Sarah Pinborough)
*"Fix"** (with J. Konrath & Ann Voss Peterson)

The ICE Trilogy*

Panacea
The God Gene
The Void Protocol

The Nocturnia Chronicles
(with Thomas F. Monteleone)

Definitely Not Kansas
Family Secrets
The Silent Ones

Short Fiction

Soft & Others
The Barrens and Others
Aftershock and Others
The Christmas Thingy
*Quick Fixes—Tales of Repairman Jack**
Sex Slaves of the Dragon Tong
Secret Stories

Editor

Freak Show
Diagnosis: Terminal
The Hogben Chronicles (with Pierce Watters)

* See "The Secret History of the World" (Page 175)

SUNDAY—MAY 14

Barbara

1

Ellie was changed when she came out of the coma.

Not that I expected the exact same flaky, sixteen-year-old we'd all known and loved, not after she'd been dead to the world between Christmas and May Day, all the while constantly shuttled in and out of a hyperbaric chamber to help heal her burns. The doctors warned me that some cognitive changes were inevitable.

But this was something else. This was some*one* else.

She awoke looking just like her sixteen-year-old self–the same straight black hair, the same round face and pale skin. But she wasn't really Ellie. Not anymore.

Someone else looked out through her owlish blue eyes.

Perhaps I should have suspected things weren't quite right when her burns started to heal, but I was too happy to imagine any sort of downside. I mean, third-degree burns aren't supposed to heal. They run the full thickness of the skin and beyond, down to the fatty layer and sometimes through that and into the underlying muscle. They require tissue grafts to fill in and skin grafts to close.

But Ellie's burns started filling in by themselves as fresh new skin–*skin*, not scar tissue–slowly irised in from the periphery. It bothered the doctors because they couldn't explain it, but I was ecstatic. My Ellie wouldn't be horribly scarred for life.

I'd been with her every day. I'd even brought Blanky–yes, that's what she still called the ratty old blanket she'd kept since childhood and slept with every night, even as a teen–and I kept it by her side.

And then in early May she came to. Like someone awakening from a nap, she opened her eyes and said, "I want to go home."

No disorientation, no asking what had happened. It seemed as if she'd been aware all along.

As I looked at her I felt my initial burst of joy wither in the cold certainty that Ellie wasn't back. Not really. Not *my* Ellie.

As I was hustled out of the unit by the nurses flocking around her, I heard her voice rise about the hubbub: "Mother? Mother, did you hear me? I want to go home!"

Ellie has never called me "Mother." Never.

I stood in the doorway, staring back at my younger daughter, and thinking this has to be the strangest moment of my life. But I was wrong. So, so wrong. Things hadn't begun to get strange.

Shaken and sweaty, I retreated to the waiting room and relived that week in December, looking for a clue as to when things had started to go wrong.

2

Bess had begged us to spend Christmas week in the city.

"It's the best time to be in New York," she'd said.

"The city's beautiful," she'd said.

"You'll love it," she'd said.

Why, oh, why, did I listen?

Bess was a second-year student at NYU. She'd always dreamed of attending college in Greenwich Village, though how a girl from rural Missouri got that idea into her head I'll never know. Maybe it came from devouring the Beat poets like Ginsberg and Corso. Maybe from incessantly playing Dylan's early albums. She knew well that the Village of the Beat Generation was long gone, but still she wanted to be there.

Ellie missed her older sister and loved New York almost as much as Bess, but for different reasons. The Museum of Natural History was like Mecca to her, and a trip to NYC her Hajj.

So we decided to make it a major holiday outing. Bess used Airbnb to secure us a ten-day rental on a two-bedroom apartment in the East Seventies that perfectly suited our needs. We cabbed in from JFK on Thursday the 18th to find Bess waiting for us at the front door. We all walked to the local Gristedes to fill the refrigerator, then went out for an early dinner at a little Tex-Mex place on Second Avenue.

How different my two girls. Bess takes after me: long-faced, wavy, honey-blonde hair, brown-eyed, a bit on the plump side, but pleasingly so, I like to think. Ellie is lanky with a round face, straight black hair, and can't stand contacts so is never without her owlish tortoise shell rims. Bess fancies herself a Bohemian, while Ellie the scientist turns her nose up at "artsy-fartsy stuff."

After dinner Bess left us to return to her dorm and Ellie and I went to bed. The start of what looked to be a perfect family trip. If I'd had any hint of what was coming, I'd have packed us up right then and caught the next non-stop back to St. Louis.

I've always gotten along well with my two daughters, but we've become especially close since Ray's sudden death five years ago. He was stopped at a railroad crossing when a texting teenage girl rear-ended him and pushed his car into the path of the oncoming freight train. He died instantly. Over the years he'd made a fairly good living as an insurance salesman and, true to his own sales pitches-and taking advantage of his employee discount-he'd accumulated a number of valuable term policies on himself. His death benefit came to a little over three and a half million dollars.

So financially, he left us very well off, though I'm sure the girls would much prefer to have their father around instead. I take a different view. I've never told them that one of the clerks at the coroner's office-an old rival from the high school cheering squad-made sure I overheard her mention that when they extricated the bodies from the car, Ray's young secretary, killed along with him, was found with her face buried in his lap.

I wasn't all that surprised. So as a consequence I've managed to find perfect contentment in the money, and spend it lavishly on the girls.

In New York, the first hint of the strangeness that lurked ahead came the very next day as we cabbed down to Washington Square Park to meet Bess for a personalized tour of the Village. We were making our way along Fifth Avenue past the lower reaches of Central Park when Ellie, who'd been immersed in Snapchat with her friends back home, suddenly straightened and looked around, her blue eyes wide behind her round glasses.

"What is *that*?" she said.

"What's what, honey?"

"That noise."

I listened but heard nothing beyond typical traffic sounds.

"I'm sorry. I don't hear anything special. What's it sound like?"

Her expression turned annoyed. "You really can't hear it?"

"Hear what?"

She rolled down the window, letting in the cool air. "*Now* do you hear it?"

I shook my head. "Sorry."

After a frustrated growl, she said, "It's like a hum but real loud and real low, you know like those bass beats when Phil Oliver drives by with his rap blasting?"

I knew. Thumping notes so loud and low you felt them as well as heard them, even when his windows were up.

"Got it."

"Okay, it's like that, only steady–one steady note."

I strained my ears but finally had to shrug. "Sorry."

Another growl, and then the driver rapped on the Plexiglas partition between front and back seats.

"Maybe you hear Balto," he said, grinning.

The license info taped to the divider said his name was Zarim Sheikh, but his English was good and obviously he'd been listening.

"Who's Balto?" Ellie said.

"A hero dog who helped children." He pointed into the park. "He has statue past those trees."

"That's right where the noise is coming from." Smirking, she turned to me. "See? He hears it too. So I'm not crazy."

"No, miss," he said. "I do not hear this noise."

She pressed her hands over her ears. "It's so *loud*, how can anyone *not*?"

I surveyed the pedestrians on this chill December morning, but none seemed bothered in the least as they bustled along on the sidewalk that bordered the park.

I felt a twinge of unease as I watched Ellie sit there holding her ears in such obvious distress. When I was a child my Aunt Tilda used to hear things–voices and such. Her doctor called them auditory hallucinations, but they were part of her diagnosis of schizophrenia. Did it run in the family? Was this the first sign that Ellie was losing her mind?

For years we'd playfully called Ellie "our little weirdo." Not because she truly believed in flying saucers and alien abductions and Sasquatch and Nessie and all the rest. She didn't. She was super rational, but she *wanted* those stories to be true. She studied TV and Internet accounts, looking for irrefutable evidence. She was the living, breathing embodiment of that X-Files line, *I want to believe!*

Were those quirks also aspects of some sort of mental illness that had now evolved into auditory hallucinations?

As we moved farther downtown, she removed her hands from her ears.

"It seems to be fading a bit." She craned her neck to look at the park. "It's a little behind us now. Definitely from the park."

As we neared the end of the park, she tapped on the partition.

"Mister Taximan, can you turn right, please?"

"But Washington Square is straight ahead," he said. "At the very end of Fifth Avenue."

She turned to me. "Mom, can we? Can we? The noise is over that way."

She seemed so anxious and I didn't see how it could hurt.

"Go ahead, driver," I said.

So we turned onto Central Park South, past the Plaza Hotel to our left and the line of handsome cabs with their huffing horses on our right. Even if they'd all been out with fares, their smell was unmistakable.

"See, it's getting louder now," she said, "but not as loud as before. Louder...louder..."

But as before, I heard nothing and, as far as I could tell, neither did anybody else on the crowded sidewalks. As we passed Seventh Avenue, she pointed straight uptown into the park.

"It's right in there somewhere–right *there*!"

For a moment I was afraid she'd jump out of the cab, but then I realized hearing the noise disturbed her as much as not hearing it disturbed me.

And then, with a look of profound relief, she lowered her hands and looked around.

"It's stopped! Whatever it was, it's gone. Just like that." She turned to me. "What was it, Mom? How come only I could hear it?"

"I haven't the faintest idea, honey."

I didn't see how I could tell her my greatest fear. But I might as well have, because schizophrenia would have been a blessing compared to what was to come.

3

We spent a wonderful weekend around the city–including the
Museum of Natural History, of course–topping it off with a Sunday
matinee of *The Lion King* followed by dinner at Bond 45 in the the-
ater district. Then, on Monday morning, Ellie announced that she
wanted to visit the Balto statue. She'd heard the cab driver mention
it, looked it up, and decided she wanted to see it in person.

At least that was what she told me.

Bess thought it a dumb idea, especially with a major snowstorm
due the next day. But when I suggested we visit the zoo after Balto,
then ride on the carousel before lunching at Tavern-on-the-Green,
she agreed to meet us on Fifth Avenue.

We entered the park near Sixty-seventh Street and Ellie used a
Central Park walking tour app on her phone to lead us to Balto. The
bronze statue of the famous huskie stood high on a rock outcropping
where a plaque told the story of how, back in 1925, he guided a sled
team through an Alaskan blizzard to deliver diphtheria antitoxin to
a group of sick children.

But despite the fact that this had been her idea, Ellie didn't seem
the least bit interested in Balto. In fact she kept her back to the
statue while she stared at her phone. I had a feeling she wasn't on
Snapchat...

Bess said, "Okay, why don't we head for the zoo now? It's just–"

"I want to go this way," Ellie said, pointing deeper into the park.
"There's someplace I need to see."

"Are you kidding?" Bess said. "I'm f-f-freezing!"

Bess had a bit of drama queen in her. Being cold was her own
fault. Despite the chilly temperatures, she'd arrived dressed in an
NYU hoodie. She could have been comfy warm in the Patagonia
Micro-Puff jacket I'd bought her but I'm sure she felt it lacked suf-
ficient bo-ho cred.

I had a gut feeling about Ellie, though...

"Is this about–?"

"The sound," she said, nodding, her look pleading. "I need to see
where it came from. Please?"

We'd had such a nice trip so far, I figured I'd indulge her. We had
no schedule, after all.

Of course Bess wanted to know "What sound?" and, as we followed Ellie, I explained the episode on Friday as best I could.

"That's not normal, Mom," Bess whispered.

"But it's not necessarily bad. Maybe her ears are just...different."
I wanted so very much to believe that.

Ellie led us this way and that way along intersecting paths and across the wide, bench-lined mall that seems to pop up in so many films set in Manhattan, past volleyball courts, and then into a wide-open field.

"This is called the Sheep Meadow," Ellie announced, continuing to the center where she stopped and pointed downtown toward the apartment buildings and hotels that lined Central Park South. "And right down there is where Seventh Avenue stops."

"So?" Bess said.

"So this is where I think the sound came from. At least it's my best guess."

Bess made a face. "That doesn't make any sense. There's nothing around but grass. Unless someone drove a speaker system into the middle here and started broadcasting a sound only weirdoes can hear–"

Ellie screamed then. A piercing, agonized sound ripped from her throat as her face paled and I swear her sneakers lifted a foot off the turf. She dropped her phone and clapped her hands over her ears and took off at a dead run, screaming all the while. With shock and terror spiking my chest, I chased after her, Bess close behind.

Ellie slowed when she reached a pathway at the far edge of the Sheep Meadow and staggered in a circle with a finger jammed into each ear.

As Bess and I approached she turned toward me and shouted, "Don't tell me you can't hear it *now*?"

Her distress was so genuine, and I felt so helpless.

"I don't know what else to tell you, Ellie. I don't hear anything." I turned to Bess. "Do you?"

She shook her head. "I hear the traffic up on the street but that's all. What's it sound like?"

"Like a moan–a long moan that never stops. And so *loud!* Not as loud as it was back in the field, but–" She jammed her hands over her ears again. "I can't *stand* it!"

I hovered beside her. "I don't know what to do!"

"Make it stop. Please, Mom, you've got to make it stop!"

"We can't hear it, Ellie. That means it's in your head. Does covering your ears help?"

"No, it's all around."

A man had trotted up and skidded to a stop before her.

"You hear it too?" he said, staring.

Ellie nodded as her face paled further, and her cheeks...they seemed to be sinking.

I looked at the man–tall and wiry with ruddy skin, high cheekbones, and a sharp nose. He looked Indian–not the Hindu kind, the Native American kind. If he heard it, that meant it wasn't just in Ellie's head, not some mental aberration.

"It's making me sick. I wanna go home!"

"You mean like back to Mizzou?" Bess said.

Ellie retched. "I'm gonna puke!"

"No, don't! You know I hate that smell. It makes *me* wanna puke!"

"Hush, Bess!" I said. This wasn't about her.

The man started to turn away. He looked like he was in pain–from the sound?

And then, as she'd warned, Ellie vomited–not her breakfast but a long stream of bright red blood.

"Oh, no!" I cried, horrified. "Ellie, no!"

She dropped to her knees and did it again. So much blood...

And then she fell onto her side, but never took her hands off her ears.

"Make it stop, Mom," she gasped, her face so white. "Make it stop!"

And then her eyelids fluttered and she passed out.

The stranger knelt and slipped his arms under Ellie's back and knees. As he lifted her, he said, "Call 9-1-1!"

"What are you doing?" I screamed as he started carrying her away. "Put her down!"

"The sound's not so loud up by the street," he said.

"What sound?"

"You really don't hear it?"

"No! And put her down!"

"Just follow me, lady. She'll be better on the sidewalk."

He increased his pace and I stared to scream for help.

"He's taking my little girl! Someone stop him! Please, someone stop him!"

But people simply stared. No one moved to intervene, so I ran after him.

He reached the sidewalk and darted to the nearest bench where a young couple sat staring at their phones.

"Move-move-move!" he shouted

As they jumped up and stepped away, he laid Ellie on the bench and began slapping her cheeks–gently but insistent.

"Kid? Wake up, kid. The sound's not so loud here."

I grabbed his shoulder and pulled him away, then pushed myself between them.

"Get away from her!"

"Did you call the EMTs?"

"I was too busy chasing you!"

He made a face as he pulled out his phone and stabbed at the keypad. After a few seconds he said, "Little girl vomiting blood at Sixty-Ninth and CPW," then ended the call.

A moment later, Ellie woke up.

"The noise…"

I kissed her forehead. "It's gone now?"

"No. But it not as loud. It's not making me sick anymore."

I looked up and met the stranger's concerned eyes. I realized he'd only been trying to help.

"Thank you. I'm sorry I panicked. I just–"

He shrugged and smiled. "A strange man carrying my daughter off? I'd panic too."

"But what's this sound she's talking about? I thought it was all in her head, but you seem to hear it too."

He looked from Bess to me. "And you don't? Neither of you?" When we both shook our heads he turned to the small crowd that had gathered out of nowhere. "Who here hears that noise, that loud low hum?"

Not one person raised a hand. They looked at him like he was crazy.

"What is it?" I said. "Where does it come from?"

He shrugged. "Wish I knew. Heard it Friday, now again today."

Just like Ellie…

"Thank you again. May I ask your name?"

He hesitated, then said, "Hill…Tier Hill."

Tier…an odd name. I wanted to ask him about the sound but

just then Ellie started to sob.

"What's wrong?" I said.

"It stopped! It finally stopped!"

And then she passed out again.

The police and EMTs arrived together and made me back off while they checked Ellie. I looked around for the stranger. I wanted to ask him more about what he'd heard, but he was gone. Then one of the EMTs grabbed my arm.

"That's your daughter, right?" Something hostile in her expression.

"Yes..."

"Where'd she get those burns?"

"What burns?"

"She's burned all over."

Panicked, I pushed past the police and the EMTs to Ellie's side. They had one arm out of her sleeve–to start an IV, I suppose–but her skin was covered with red, angry, inch-wide blisters. They'd pulled up her sweater to reveal her abdomen and the blisters were even bigger there.

"*What?*" I screamed. "What did you do to her?"

"That's what we were about to ask you," said a cop. "Her clothes aren't burned. She must have had those when she got dressed."

"No wonder she's passed out," said another EMT. "Those look like third-degree burns."

I couldn't take my eyes off those horrible marks. "But we just walked all the way across the park."

"Really?" said a black cop. "A woman over there says she saw a man carrying her out of the park."

No...they couldn't think...

Before I could reply, an EMT shouted, "She's going into shock. We've got to get her to a burn unit and fast!"

4

And so it went.

They raced Ellie to Columbia-Presbyterian's burn center and into its hyperbaric oxygen chamber. For a while the city's Administration for Children's Services was all over Beth and me, but video monitoring around the park showed Ellie in no distress at the Balto statue, so they eventually let us be.

No one ever figured out the origin of her burns. I mentioned the sound in the Sheep Meadow that only Ellie could hear as a possible source, but this earned me suspicious looks that I knew would eventually graduate to questions about my fitness as a mother if I persisted, so I zipped my lips.

The burn center—officially the William Randolph Hearst Burn Center—wasn't in Washington Heights at the main Columbia-Pres location, but on East Sixty-eighth Street, not too many blocks from our Airbnb place. *Way* east. Past York Avenue. Any farther on and it would have been floating on the East River.

I stayed there for days straight. Not that I had much choice at first, what with the predicted "Snowmageddon" blizzard shutting down the city, but I wasn't leaving Ellie's side until I knew she was going to live.

Finally they gave me the word that her blood pressure and other vital signs had stabilized. The big danger now was sepsis. If they could keep her burns free from infection, she'd make it, although she faced a very long road to recovery.

I extended the Airbnb rental to six months and made the walk back and forth to York Avenue every day. The regular exercise and eating hospital caf food left no mystery as to why I lost weight. Not so Ellie's burns, however. The mystery of how they healed without scars was never solved. No one could explain it, just as no one could explain her extended coma either. She had no brain damage, her brain waves were perfectly normal, yet none of the hotshot neurologists could bring her out of it.

Nor could they explain the strange proclamations she'd occasionally shout out at the top of her lungs.

Twilight has come…night will follow…

That was a favorite of hers. We heard it over and over.

It will begin in the heavens and end in the Earth was another fave, sometimes—but not always—followed by, *But before that, the rules will be broken.*

Winter passed and spring arrived without her knowledge, and then, on May 14, nineteen weeks after falling into a coma, Ellie opened her eyes and spoke.

I called Bess and she cried when she heard the news. She said she'd be up right after a seminar.

When the initial hubbub attendant to Ellie's awakening passed, they let me back in to see her. I took her hand and she stared at me with those not-Ellie eyes.

"I have to get home," she said in a perfectly clear voice. "I have something I must do."

"I hope you don't mean home to Missouri," I said. "You're not finished here. You need lots of rehab to tone up your muscles. You haven't used them in months and they're weak."

She gave my hand a painful squeeze. "Does that feel weak? I don't need rehab; I need out of here. I don't need our home home, the apartment will do fine, but I need to build."

"Build what?"

"A shelter."

"I don't understand." And I didn't. Truly.

"You will," she said with a disturbing finality.

I tried to talk about what had gone on in the world while she was out of it, but she didn't care.

"It doesn't matter, Mother," she said. *Mother*...the unfamiliar word from Ellie's lips gave me the creeps. "None of it matters. Twilight has come. Night will follow. That's all we need to know."

"You've been saying that for months. What does it *mean*? I don't understand."

"You will."

The bed was needed for a fireman recovering from burns, so they came to move Ellie to a semi-private room. I took the opportunity to step out for a bite to eat. I'd been making an occasional stop at this sushi place on First Avenue, so I walked there, hoping it was open on a Sunday. It was. I ordered a nigiri platter and had a second glass of wine to celebrate Ellie's recovery. I felt as if I should be celebrating. I figured I was supposed to. After all, my daughter was back from a coma, wasn't she?

But *was* it my daughter?

Of course it was, I told myself. How could it be anyone else?

The sudden, unexpected release of the unbearable strain of all these months had me imagining things.

Yes. That sounded good.

I wished I could have believed a single word of it.

Of *course* the strain of not knowing if she'd ever wake up had been crushing. I mean, how could these doctors bring her back to consciousness if none of them could say why she was *un*conscious?

Well, she was conscious now–or at least *someone* was conscious. But that change in her eyes…it sounds so tenuous, so vapid, so insubstantial, so *stupid* when I put it into words, but a mother knows her daughter, and that girl in the hospital…nope…not my Ellie.

I finished my half-dozen sushi pieces and stepped out into the spring air. As I started back toward the medical center I saw a teenager walking toward me. Something so familiar about her gait. And then I realized…

"Ellie! What–?"

"Oh, hello, Mother." Calm, collected, and as cool as can be. "I told you I had to get out of there."

She didn't even pause as she came abreast of me, just kept walking. She had Blanky tied around her neck like a cape.

"But where…?" I pointed to her bare feet and baggy jeans and Hofstra T-shirt.

"Borrowed from my new roommate. She won't miss them for a while."

I fell into step beside her. "But what about rehab?"

"Do I look like I need rehab?"

I had to admit to myself that she didn't. She'd lost weight during the ordeal–we both had–but I'd had excess pounds to lose, not her.

"But the doctors–"

"–can pound salt. I–oooh, looky here."

She stopped short and stared at a pair of garbage cans filled with carpentry scraps sitting by the curb. Someone was renovating.

She started pulling out lengths of two-by-four and molding and handing them to me.

"Hold these."

She dug further and pulled out some galvanized metal strips. These she kept herself as she started walking again.

"I'm going to need some supplies," she said. "I'll need a hammer, nails, screws, a cordless drill, some of that Gorilla Glue, a soldering iron, oh, and a protractor."

"Why on Earth…?"

"I told you: I need to build a shelter."

Hari

"Your skills may prove crucial to my future, and to yours as well."

Yeah, right, Hari thought as she stopped before a Chelsea townhouse on West Twenty-first Street. Her "skills" were with numbers-specifically forensic accounting.

Seeing a client on a Sunday was no big deal-she worked seven days a week, after all-but a house call? Normally she didn't visit a client's home unless big bucks were in the offing, but this fellow had all but begged her, saying no way could he come to her. She'd considered blowing him off, but his address was between Seventh and Eighth Avenues, a short, tree-lined walk from her office in the Flatiron District, and the May day was mild and sunny, so why not?

The tall, narrow, Victorian row house dressed in dark brown stone loomed behind a low, wrought-iron fence. Each floor had its own large bay window. A tiny patch of lawn sat on either side of the short slate walk leading to the front steps.

Wouldn't mind living here, she thought as she climbed the steps and rang the doorbell. Back in the seventies, when NYC was on the on the verge of default, these things could be had for a song. Now they went for millions.

A long-haired twenty-something wearing jeans and a red T emblazoned with $i > u$ opened the door. He'd affected that three-millimeter facial stubble that guys in his generation thought so cool. Hari wrote it off to clueless trendiness.

"Don't tell me you're Arthur Palaez," she said.

He grinned. "No way. I'm Donny Tuite, his assistant."

"'Tweet'? As in what you do on Twitter?"

"Not even close." He spelled it for her.

She stuck out her hand. "Hari Tate. Your boss and I have a ten o'clock appointment."

"Really? Oh, man. When Art said a Harry Tate would be stopping by-"

"-you expected a guy."

"Right."

He wasn't a good liar. In her line of work Hari ran into lots of really good liars–accountants who cooked books for a living numbered among the best–and she'd developed a feel for falsehoods. Donny had known her gender. Why pretend he hadn't?

She forced a smile. "You're not the first. Are you going to ask me in or are we just going to stand here flapping our gums?"

"Oh, yeah, no, come on in."

Another set of oak doors, these adorned with frosted glass designs, divided the tiny vestibule from the rest of the house. She followed Donny through to the oak paneled foyer. A long narrow staircase ran up along the wall to her right. An ornate chandelier, festooned with heavy red glass grapes, hung overhead. Far to the rear, daylight filtered in through tall windows overlooking a courtyard.

"I should be wearing your T-shirt," Hari said.

His gaze dropped to her breasts and lingered. She'd been working on dropping some weight and was actually getting her waist back, but still had a ways to go. The good thing was her bust hadn't shrunk.

"I don't know if it would fit."

"Maybe not, but I think it might be more accurate."

He grinned–he had a nice smile. "I think I like you."

"You'll get over it."

He pressed a button on an intercom/alarm panel to the left and said, "Ms. Tate is here."

"Be right down."

Donny turned to her. "He'll be right down."

"No kidding? Right down? Thanks for telling me. I never would have known."

She wanted to pull the words back. Dial it down a bit, Hari. Her ex had told her she needed anger-management training. She didn't think so. She just needed fewer people saying dumb things.

Also, she was low on caffeine.

But he just laughed. "You're a tough one, but I guess that was–what would you call it?"

"How about redundant?"

"Nailed it. Captain Redundant."

She kind of liked Donny. Except for the stubble and the white lie about expecting a guy, he seemed genuine, comfortable in his skin.

She tried to make nice-nice.

"I like these old places," she said, looking around. "They've got character."

"This one's got some history. Back in the fifties and sixties it was divided into apartments–one to a floor. Then a psychiatrist named Gates bought it and totally restored it. He lived here until just a couple of years ago when he blew a hole through his head in Times Square. Nobody knows why but there must have been something hinky going on because he left the place to one of his patients."

"I guess you'd call that a close doctor-patient relationship."

"I guess, right? Anyway, the patient had an accident here and didn't want to stay, so she put it up for sale almost immediately. Art came along and snapped it up."

Right on cue, a slim, olive-skinned man of about forty descended the stairs and thrust out his hand.

"Arthur Palaez."

Hari introduced herself, and Arthur–"call me Art"–offered coffee which Hari could not refuse. The meeting would go much more smoothly if she was properly caffeinated. She told Donny she took it black. As he went off to make some fresh, she followed Art as he bounded up the stairs to the second floor.

"When you said you couldn't come to my office," Hari said, puffing, "I assumed you were disabled in some way."

"I am," he said, tapping a finger against his temple. "Agoraphobia. I totally flip out if I have to leave the house. I do so only for the direst emergencies. But tell me about you. Indian? Pakistani? Bangladeshi?"

Seriously?

"Han Chinese–pure bred."

He blinked. "Pardon?"

Oh, hell. "My grandparents were from Mumbai. Does it matter?"

"I just like to be aware so I don't tread on any cultural differences."

"I'll take a load off your mind: I'm American. Born and raised in Mineola."

"I guess I was also asking because Tate isn't exactly a Mumbai-ish name."

"I took it from Mister Tate when we married and kept if after he left. Fits a lot better on a business card that Mukhopadhyay."

Art cringed a little. "I'll say."

My turn.

"As long as we're being all ethno-sensitive, you're a Spaniard, I take it?"

"Asturian, to be precise. It's a little principality in the-"

Hari waved a hand. "'Spain' is good enough." She looked around at nearly a dozen flat screen monitors of various sizes arrayed under the fifteen-foot ceiling, all dancing with graphs and banners except for Fox Business News on one, CNBC on another, Bloomberg on still another. "So why does a day trader-I'm assuming that's your game- need a forensic accountant?"

He indicated a chair and they both seated themselves.

"I'm interested in the activities of a very small brokerage house called Sedam."

"Never heard of it."

"Neither has anyone else. They have only one client: The Ancient Septimus Fraternal Order Foundation."

"Septimus...aren't they like the Masons or something like that?"

Art shrugged. "I guess. They say they go way back before Mesopotamia, but really, who's going to buy that? Anyway, what interests me about their brokerage house is that it's tres conservative. They deal mostly in Spiders. But back in February, early in the month, they began quietly buying puts in the tech sector-*lots* of puts: Twitter, Microsoft, Facebook, Google, Snapchat, anything that relied on the Internet."

He stopped and his gaze bore into Hari as he let that sink in.

Hari knew immediately where he was going.

Back in February, a mystery camorra launched violent assaults on the Internet's infrastructure. The attacks were coordinated with the emergence of the so-called Jihadi virus that ran wild across the globe, creating a botnet that crashed the worldwide system.

If Art was to be believed, just before the crash this Sedam brokerage had switched from safe and sane SPDRs to puts on Internet stocks...option bets that those stocks would go down. And of course, they did, following the Internet into the abyss. The net remained thoroughly trashed for days, followed by a week or two of limping improvement. The experts were still crunching the numbers, but the resulting financial loss was estimated at somewhere between one hundred and two hundred billion dollars. Now, three months later, things were back to some semblance of order, but the crash had caused global chaos.

Coincidence?

"That can only mean they knew the crash was coming," she said.

Art's expression was grim as he nodded. "'Twould seem so."

Did he just say *'twould*?

"So with all those Internet stocks in the toilet, this Sedam place cleaned up."

"*Really* cleaned up."

Donny arrived with the coffee then, adding, "Sort of like all the puts bought on United and American Airlines before the 9/11 attack."

Hari had heard stories about that, but didn't know if they were true or not.

She sipped her much-needed coffee–*excellent*.

"Donny," she said, "if Art ever lets you go, you can come work for me–just so you can make coffee."

"Deal!" Donny said.

"Really?" Art looked offended.

Donny grinned. "But she's so much better looking than you, Art."

Hari took that as a compliment, but looking at Art, she wasn't so sure.

"Okay," she said, "I'm guessing you want to look into those options, but why do you want me doing the looking?"

Art frowned. "Sorry?"

"Lots of forensic accountants around. Why me?"

"Oh, that was Donny."

Well, now, this was interesting.

Donny reddened a bit and fumbled out, "Yeah, well, I asked around and someone said, 'Get Tate. Tate is great.'"

This guy couldn't lie to save his life. Something going on here, but Art didn't seem a part of it. All Donny...

Hari decided to play along for now, see if she could suss out Donny's game.

"'Tate is Great,'" she said. "Has a nice ring to it." To Art: "What are you hoping to gain from my looking into those options?"

"Oh, those aren't my concern," he said. "I'm more concerned with Sedam's current activities. You see, after cleaning up on the Internet crash, they went back to their Spiders, but only for a month. Starting early April they began selling off all their holdings–*all* their holdings. They're doing it discreetly, so as not to draw attention, but I've no doubt they're doing it."

"And you know this how?"

He glanced at Donny. "I can't say. Just let me be clear that there's no question they're liquidating."

Okay, he'd hacked them.

Hari shrugged. "So what? What do you care?"

Art leaned forward, his expression grim. "I wouldn't care in the least if I didn't know about their February puts. But I do. They were betting on something happening to the Internet. And something did: one of the biggest social, commercial, and communications disasters ever. If the computer geeks hadn't been able to fix it so fast, I'd be selling apples on the street–and I don't mean MacBooks."

The Internet crash...just three months ago. Every business in the world had been affected, including Hari's. Amazing how fast they'd repaired or replaced the damaged fiber-optic cables and disrupted the botnet by developing a fix for the Jihad virus. In a matter of only a few days much of the Word Wide Web was back up and running. Not without glitches and bandwidth problems, not business as usual by any means, but people were able to begin to get things done again.

"So...you're wondering if they've got some insider info on another calamity?"

"'Calamity' might be too gentle a word for it. Catastrophe? Cataclysm? *Apocalypse?* They're no longer working an angle to profit from the market, they're getting *out* of the market. Does that mean they suspect that *all* stocks will soon be worthless? If so, I want to know–I *must* know."

Hari shook her head. "I don't see how a forensic accountant can help you with that."

"Indirectly, you can. Sedam brokerage is moving to cash, and that cash is, in turn, moving to its source: the Septimus Foundation. But where's the cash going from there? They can't be storing it in a vault–they've got to be spending it. But on what? Krugerrands? Soybeans? Rare single malts? If I know that, I'll have a clue as to what they think will happen."

"How do you know *anything's* going to happen?"

"I don't. But *I* want to know what *they* know, and then I'll make my own decision."

"I don't know..." Hari said.

And she didn't. This did not seem to be in her bailiwick.

"One week," Art said. "Give me one week and I'll pay you one hundred K. In advance. If you solve it in less than one week or even if you don't solve it at all, the hundred-K is still yours."

A hundred thousand for a week's work...her hourly billable rate was high, but no way she'd ever amass that number of hours in a week. But first offers were rarely the final offer. Could she goose a boost?

"Tempting..." she said slowly.

"One fifty," he said. "That's my final offer. And don't forget: The answer to my question could have a big impact on your future as well."

"I might have expenses, like travel and such."

Hey, if you don't ask...

"I'll give Donny a credit card to charge what you need–within reason, of course."

Okay, nice to know what she was worth to this guy, but time to be up front.

"I'd love to take your money, Art, but I don't know if I can deliver. You're in no position to get a court order to make this Septimus Foundation open its books to me, and they aren't going to do it because of my good looks and scintillating personality. The only option is hacking their in-house system and that's–"

"–illegal?" Art said with a smile. "Donny's already done it."

Just as she'd suspected. "Donny?"

"The kid's an ace. We've been in for a while but it's a messy maze in there. We need someone who knows what they're looking at."

Hari had a thing about privacy. An almost extinct concept now, but that didn't diminish her reverence for it. Still, Art was talking about a group that had profited from the Internet outage–which might mean they'd been party to it. That put them on the Hari Tate shit list. A long list, to be sure, but always room for one more.

Her job was to study a pile of numbers and know what she was looking at when people didn't want her to know what she was looking at.

She nodded slowly. "Might be worth a try."

"Super!" Art said. "And since it's our hack, you'll be working from here."

"Oh, no. I need my office staff to–"

Art shook his head. "In the course of trying to do this on our own, we've learned some stuff about Septimus. They're not nice people."

"'Not nice' how?"

Donny spoke up. "For one thing, they've become pretty cozy with the Kickers lately. They've got their own security people, but the Kickers seem to act as their Brown Shirts."

Kickers...everyone knew the Kickers. Supposedly a self-realization group, but it seemed to Hari most of its members had a knack for embracing their inner thug. Rumor had it they'd contributed to the Internet outage by helping to damage its infrastructure, but nothing had been proven.

"For safety sake," Art said, "everything's got to stay under one roof–this one."

Hari considered: her office was only a few blocks away...she'd be tied up for a week tops...she could have some of her associates service her other clients during that time.

She gestured around. "Doesn't seem to be room enough here for the three of us."

"You'll be working with Donny in the basement."

"All right." She turned to Donny. "Show me what you've got."

Along the way they stopped in the kitchen so Hari could get a coffee refill and she noted with approval that Donny used a French press.

"So..." she said. "You're the in-house hacker?"

She expected some dodgery, but he nodded immediately and said, "Yep."

"Exclusively for Art?"

"Lately, yeah. Used to be an on-and-off thing, but now he's got a bug up his butt about this Sedam brokerage and the Septimus Foundation and what they know and what they're up to."

"In a nutshell," Hari said, "what do *we* know about what *they* know–so far?"

"Well, for one thing–"

"Let's take this downstairs so I can see if your man cave is going to work for me."

She wanted to get him out of earshot of Art.

He opened a door that led off the kitchen and motioned her to follow.

As they descended the steps he picked up where he'd left off. "We know they're spending their cash and not keeping good financial records."

"Even a charitable foundation's got to keep records–to show where the money's coming from and where it's going. Else the IRS'll getcha."

"They used to keep great records. I mean, their past records are as scrupulous as all hell, as if they were terrified of an audit. But now it's like they don't give a shit. Almost as if they're not worried about an audit. Like it's never gonna happen. And that's got Art worried. To be perfectly honest, I'm a little worried myself."

Hari wasn't crazy about it either. The Septimus order had won its bets on the Internet meltdown. Were they expecting a civilization meltdown next?

"But that's not the strangest thing I found," he said as they reached bottom. "Come over here and I'll show you."

Hari followed him across the basement to where two rolling desk chairs sat before a counter supporting three monitors. Donny held a seat for Hari.

"Appreciated," she said as she sat, "but that's the last time you do that, okay?"

"Gotcha."

He dropped into the other chair and moused a monitor to life.

"I did some editing in advance to bring you up to speed. Since I can't make sense of their financials–that's why *you're* here–I've been delving into–"

"Let's hold it right there on why I'm here. I want to hear something a little more truthful than that 'Tate is great' bullshit and how you didn't know I was female."

He reddened again. "How did you know?"

"I'd love to play poker with you sometime."

He shook his head. "Yeah, I really suck at poker. Okay, I'll give you the skinny, but you might not want to hear it."

"I'm wearing my big-girl panties. I can handle it."

He took a breath. "I hang out on the dark web. That's like my employment agency."

"There really is such a thing?"

"For sure. I can't exactly advertise my hacking services on Craigslist, so...anyway, last fall your name came up in a chatroom about getting too close to piercing a legend some powerful folks would have preferred you leave alone. They were talking about making a move against you if you kept poking, but apparently you stopped. They were pretty impressed with how far you'd penetrated, but they weren't going to let you get any deeper."

Last fall...she remembered being hired by a guy named Stahlman to check out the defunct Modern Motherhood Clinics and–coincidentally–the foundation behind them. She'd discovered that the foundation was a shell and the woman who had fronted the clinics was a bogus identity with a skillfully constructed legend. Hari would have dug deeper had Stahlman requested it, but apparently that had proved enough for him.

"How would they have stopped me?"

"The dark web is a gathering place for hackers like me, but also less savory types–like pedophiles and bomb makers and, well, hitmen." Donny held up a hand. "I know you're going to try to laugh it off, but there are more button men out there on the dark web than you want to believe. It's perfect for them. They don't know who hires them, the contractors don't know who they hire, the hitters have no connection to the victim, and they're paid with bitcoins or some other cryptocurrency."

They were talking about making a move against you...

A chill rippled along Hari's back. At least she was long past that investigation, but still...she'd had no idea...

"Sorry you had to hear that," he added, "but you insisted."

"I did, didn't I." She shook it off. "Whatever. Let's get back to these emails."

"Right. For two months now these Septimus Foundation folks have been obsessing about 'signals' and 'frequencies' and 'wavelengths' and stuff like that."

Hari swirled her cooling coffee and watched the screen. Emails flashed by too fast to read.

"Slow down."

"Most of these are complete bores but they're available if you want to go back later. I rewound to the first of the year and started

from there. Nobody mentions signals or frequencies until February–
right after the Internet crash. That's when you start seeing mentions
like these."

The stream stopped on an email with a yellow-highlighted excerpt.

"*The signal frequencies are changing again!*"

Followed by another.

"*Synchronization is coming!*"

and

"*Soon-soon-soon!*"

"Look at all those exclamation points," Hari said. "They sound
excited. Could 'synchronization' and 'frequencies' be code words?"

Donny shook his head. "I'm not getting that feeling. But whatever
they're talking about, it petered out a week later when the Internet
started coming back to life."

"I thought you said they were obsessed."

"Stay with me here. The mentions come back in a rush at the end
of March. All of a sudden that's all they're talking about. And they
keep on talking about it. It seems they were getting some sort of
report on the signal frequencies every month, but then last month it
switched to weekly, and just last week it went daily, and *that* made
them totally giddy."

"*The high frequencies are slowing more and more!*"

"*Is it wrong to say they're slowing faster? ;-)*"

"*Not too long before they synchronize with the Prime Frequency!*"

"*I almost wish they'd take more time! We're behind schedule!*"

"*We'll be ready when synchronization comes, don't you worry!*"

"What signals?" Hari said.

Donny shrugged. "Beats the hell out of me. All I can figure is
their weekly reports on some kind of mysterious signals say they're
changing their frequencies, getting closer and closer to matching
their wavelengths to some 'prime frequency.' And when they synchronize–*bam!*–it happens."

"But we don't know what 'it' is."

"Not yet. These emails are like listening to a sibling conversation. I used to have friends who were brothers. They'd have conver-
sations using reference points that they knew and assumed I knew.
But if I came half a minute late to the conversation, I'd have no idea
they were talking about."

"Where are these frequency reports coming from?"

"That's what's been driving me crazy. They don't make any sense. Just locations and numbers in megahertz and the like."

"But the emails have to have a return address."

"Yeah: *Burbank@theallard.com.*"

"The Allard? That big old apartment building?"

"I'm guessing. And the numbers in those emails show all the wavelengths getting closer and closer to their so-called Prime Frequency."

Hari leaned back and stared at the screen. "Do you get the feeling that whatever comes with synchronization will be good for them and bad for us?"

"I do," he said, nodding. "Very much so."

She sighed. "I still don't see how I can help. Especially if, as you say, they're being very sloppy with their bookkeeping. I can ferret out false entries and double entries, but there's not a lot to be gleaned from *no* entries."

Donny stepped over to the bottom of the stairs and looked up. He seemed to be checking to see if the door was closed. He returned to the bench and cleared his throat.

"Look," he said, lowering his voice. "There's something else I'd like you to look into besides where the cash is going."

Now we're getting to it, Hari thought. Here's what he's been hiding.

She kept her expression neutral. "Shoot."

"The foundation was funding a hush-hush operation for months before the Net crash. And then, right before the crash, they shut it down."

"You're thinking they found what they were looking for–what they needed to cause the crash?"

"Maybe. But it's a little more personal than that. Okay, a *lot* more. I think my brother was involved in their operation."

"He's a hacker too?"

"Taught me everything I know. The day after the foundation shut down their project, Russ was found floating in the Hudson. The coroner ruled it an accidental drowning. But I know he was murdered. And I know the Septimus Foundation was behind it."

Ernst

"Was I exaggerating?" the agent said. "Was I?"

"Not in the least," Ernst Drexler said, tapping the manuscript before him on his desk.

The agent–Ernst was having the damnedest time recalling his name–Kushner, was it? Yes, Richard Kushner, successful literary agent. He was dressed in an expensive three-piece suit and wore an even more expensive-looking toupee that almost passed for real, but you could always tell.

"It's as unsettling as it is mindboggling," said Saar Slootjes, the Lodge's loremaster for the past ten years. Red haired and red bearded, he pursued a van Gogh look. His previous assignment had been at the Amsterdam lodge. His Dutch accent remained thick.

Ernst had summoned Kushner to his office with instructions to bring his client along. The client however was going to be delayed. Just as well. It gave them a chance to discuss the matter without him.

As a senior actuator, one of the long arms of the Order's Council of Seven, Ernst Drexler II had his own office here in the Septimus downtown Lodge.

Slootjes turned to Kushner. "You did well by alerting us to your client's books. I find them very upsetting."

"Well, I couldn't miss the obvious parallels to the Order in his new novel. He's tried to disguise it as the 'Octogon'–I don't know if the misspelling was intentional or not–by using an eight-pointed sigil instead of the seven points of ours. A clumsy attempt. But as soon as I saw it I knew I had to take action."

Although he'd been a member since his teens when his father introduced him to the Berlin Lodge as an acolyte, Ernst remained wonderstruck at how deeply the Order had penetrated the workaday world. Members everywhere, even among literary agents. When Kushner had become alarmed by his client's latest book, he'd alerted the loremaster and emailed him a copy.

"Yes," Slootjes said. "That novel…it's…well, it's deeply disturbing."

The loremaster seemed genuinely upset. Ernst could see why.

Kushner's client, Winslow by name, had penned an apocalyptic novel that closed with the end of human civilization, with the survivors serving as prey for the otherworldly beings that had reshaped reality to their own liking. The whole scenario was overseen by a former human transformed into a being better suited to this horrific new world. All the other humans in the ancient brotherhood–the "Octogon," as he called it–who had helped him realize this state of affairs, were abandoned to become prey as well.

The novel had parallels to the Change the Septimus Order was engineering, and Winslow depicted them as dupes who engineered their own demise.

Yes..." Slootjes said, nodding slowly. "P. Frank Winslow...who is he and how does he know what he knows–or what he thinks he knows?

Kushner shifted in his seat. "When he arrives, we can ask him. But while we're waiting I can tell you that he's a hack writer who–"

Ernst bit back a laugh. "I'm surprised to hear an agent admit his client is a hack."

"Well, that's strictly entre nous. But the truth is, I don't consider 'hack' a pejorative term, and I'm not saying he's a bad writer. He's decent enough. What I mean is that he has no aspirations to art. He simply has this seemingly bottomless well of story ideas he draws on to keep cranking out one novel after another. He finished four in various genres last year, which I sold under his own name and two pseudonyms. He's never had a bestseller and probably never will. He's what we call a midlist writer. He earns enough to live in a one-bedroom walk-up in Alphabet City. His biggest success–if you can call a series of paperback originals a success–is his continuing character named Jake Fixx, which he's milking for all it's worth."

"Did you ask him where he got all his information for his book?"

"Of course. He said from the same place he gets the ideas for all his books: from dreams."

Ernst tapped the manuscript again. "He *dreamed* this?"

"That's what he said." Kushner gave an elaborate shrug. "What can I tell you beyond that?"

"Well, if that's true," Slootjes said, his tone vehement, "then his dreams are being generated by the Enemy! Consider the takeaway from his story: That our Order–the 'Octogon' in his story–has been lied to for millennia, that they've been fooled into believing they will be put in charge when the Change comes. But they wind up as just another set of victims because the Changed world is viciously hostile to all human life. The Enemy's minions have been selling that line forever. We cannot allow this book to be published!"

"Let's not get too worked up here," Ernst said. "It's not as if this was written by some bestselling author like...like..." He snapped his fingers, blanking on the name.

"Stephen King?" Kushner offered.

"Yes, fine, Stephen King. It sounds like this Winslow has no readership worth mentioning."

"But his novel," Slootjes said, "it presents a sequence of events not unlike what we're expecting: a radical Change in the world, but with an outcome just the opposite of what we've been promised."

Clearly Slootjes was not worried about Winslow's readership. He was concerned about his own hide.

The novel's scenario had awakened one of Ernst's unspoken and long-suppressed fears: That the One and the Otherness he served had been lying to the Order all along, using its members to further its cause here in this corner of reality with no intention of delivering on the rewards so long promised.

A little late for second thoughts now, especially with the Change so close at hand.

At least according to the signals.

Their frequencies were moving toward synchronization. Not for the first time, however. They'd started progressing that way in the past only to grind to a halt.

Just then an acolyte stuck his head into the room. "There's a Mister Winslow here who says he has an appointment?"

"Show him in," Ernst said.

Slootjes's head bobbed as he muttered, "Now we'll get to the bottom of this."

Ernst sensed Slootjes's anger, but realized he was deeply afraid, and angry because of that fear.

P. Frank Winslow entered a moment later and was hardly a prepossessing figure: a slightly built man pushing forty with unruly blond hair and hazel eyes.

He came to a sudden stop when he saw the three of them.

"What's this? Feels like an ambush."

Kushner jumped up and led him to the third chair before Ernst's desk.

"No way, Frankie. Just want to hash out some potential legal problems with your novel."

"Legal?" he said, sitting.

"Yes," Slootjes said. "The 'Octogon' in your book bears a close resemblance to us–the Ancient Septimus Fraternal Order."

Winslow shrugged. "Never heard of you guys." He seemed to have a chip on his shoulder.

"Never heard of us?" Ernst said, fighting a surge of anger. Insolent pup! The Order had been born in the First Age...

"That's understandable," Slootjes said soothingly. "We do our good works in private and don't seek the limelight. It's just that the resemblance between our factual brotherhood and your fictional one is uncanny. Which brings us to these dreams Mister Kushner says form the basis for your writing. Did everything apocalyptic in this novel come from the same dream?"

Winslow shook his head. "Nah. A whole series of dreams."

"And does this organization, the 'Octogon,' play a part in all your dreams?"

"Off and on. A lot bigger part lately. That's not its name in my dreams–names don't stick with me after I'm awake so I have to make up my own. But, yeah, it's the same group of suckers."

Slootjes blinked and stiffened. "Why do you say 'suckers'?"

Winslow laughed. "Well, they've been fed this line that they're gonna be the head honchos after the world transformation goes down, and they've swallowed it hook, line, and sinker. But when the time rolls round, they're as much cannon fodder as everyone else."

"And..." Slootjes swallowed and seemed to have a hard time of it. "And the one who led them to these tragic circumstances?"

Another laugh. "That guy's a real operator. He's called 'Uno' and he gets transformed into a being who can thrive in the bad new world he's created while all his followers are left to fend for themselves. And they don't fend very well, let me tell you."

Slootjes looked sick. Ernst wasn't feeling too good himself. *Uno* and *the One*...the names could hardly be closer.

"What's this all about?" Winslow said, looking at his agent.

Kushner cleared his throat. "Well, Frankie, when I read the book, I recognized the Septimus Order as the model for the Octogon, and I sensed there might be legal trouble ahead, so I arranged this meeting to try to head it off at the pass."

Winslow jumped from his seat. "You're part of this!"

"No-no, Frankie. I'm on your side. But you've got to face the hard fact that no publisher's going to touch this if they get an inkling that a suit is waiting in the wings."

"Fuck you!" He pointed to Ernst and Slootjes in turn. "And fuck you and fuck you! You think you're gonna stop it from being published? Well, guess what? It'll be on sale tomorrow."

And then he stormed out.

"Well, thank you very much," Kushner said after the door had slammed. "There goes one of my steady earners."

Slootjes said nothing. He looked shell-shocked.

"What did he mean by that?" Ernst said. "On sale tomorrow? An empty threat, yes?"

Kushner shook his head. "Afraid not. He can self-publish it online on sites like Amazon or B-and-N or Kobo. Just a few clicks of a mouse and it can be available all over the world."

"All over the *world*?" Ernst pounded his desk. "Go catch him and bring him back."

When Kushner was gone, Slootjes looked at Ernst with haunted eyes. "What if they're true?"

"What?"

"His dreams...what if his dreams tell the future?"

The idea landed like a blow to the center of Ernst's chest. Winslow had nailed so many details about the Order itself. If his dreams about a coming apocalypse were on a par with that...

Had they all been played?

No. That sort of thinking was counterproductive. He pushed those thoughts aside.

"If his books get out to the public..." Slootjes said.

"What difference does it make? You and I are the only ones who know the story behind them. To everyone else they're pure fiction."

"But as loremaster I'm seen as an authority on the history of the Order. If our members read this book and ask me to explain the parallels, what will I tell them?"

"How can you have any doubt? You tell them it's pulp fiction and that everything is fine and going just as we've planned."

"But is it?"

This was not good. A loremaster with growing doubt about the Order's lore. Instead of providing reassurance to wavering brothers, he might instead spread panic among them. A catastrophe in the making...

The best way to avoid that was to prevent the book from being published. Which meant Winslow had to be stopped.

And Ernst knew just the man to do it.

Hari

1

...the coroner ruled it an accidental drowning...but I know he was
murdered... and I know the Septimus Foundation was behind it...

Hari ran Donny's words around in her head a few times to make
sure she had this right.

"This charitable foundation–"

"*Supposedly* charitable."

"Whatever. You're saying it murdered your brother?"

Donny's nod carried no hint of doubt. "Right."

"And you've determined this based on...?"

"Okay. I told you I accessed the foundation's spreadsheets back
to the first of the year. I also rescued a big-ass load of deleted emails.
Putting the two together, it's pretty clear that they were funding
Russ's project."

Hari held up her hands. "Stop-stop-stop. I have no idea what
you're talking about."

Donny leaned back and ran his hands through his long sandy
hair. "Of course you don't. Okay. Russ started hacking as a teen,
phreaking and the like." Before Hari could ask, he said, "Breaking
into a phone company's computers just to see if he could. Innocent
stuff."

"Why bother?"

"Just for lolz. He'd–"

"Just for *what*?"

"Lolz." He gave her an *I-can't-believe-I-have-to-explain-this*
look. "You know...for laughs."

Okay. A derivative of LOL.

"Got it. Go on."

"Okay. The worst he'd do was arrange for free long distance,
which was a big thing before cellular took over. His problem came
when he graduated to banks."

"Uh-oh," Hari said. "Ran afoul of Treasury's FinCEN unit?"

"Exactly. His hack arranged for the banks' computers to round off a fraction of a cent on each international transaction and transfer it to his Swiss account. He was collecting in the high six figures a year until someone got wise. Did two years inside but came out with a twenty-five-year ban on going online."

"Plus he was saddled with the 'felon' label."

"Right. No one wanted a felon near their computers, and computers were all he knew."

"Let me guess: He kept on hacking via the dark web."

"What choice did he have? Anyway, somewhere around the first of the year, NRO sought him out and made him an offer he couldn't refuse."

Hari held up a hand. "NRA I know. But NRO?"

"National Reconnaissance Office–one of the Big Five intelligence agencies. They run all the satellites and, as a result, their computers are under constant attack by the Russians, the Chinese, the North Koreans, Iranians, you name it. They were putting together teams of white hats and black hats to shore up their firewalls. Russ loved the work. And not only was he getting a steady check, but they promised to deep six his felony record."

"They can do that?"

Now Donny gave her an *are-you-kidding?* look. "The federal agencies have been totally off the hook for years. You wouldn't believe what I hear in the dark-web chat rooms. It's the wild west out there. But the thing is, the felony was never deep-sixed because Russ was suddenly dead. Coincidentally, another hacker from my chat room, who dropped the news that he was doing something similar but wouldn't say who for, has stopped saying anything. We haven't heard from him since early February, which was when Russ drowned."

"And you think he and Russ suffered a similar fate?"

"Let me lay out what I've put together: Russ told me their job was to take the most virulent worms and trojans the Russians and Chinese had used against the NRO's computers and make them even worse. Then they were to develop defenses against them. Once they'd done that, they were to find ways to breach *those* defenses. And then build a firewall to block *that* attack. Russ said NRO referred to their group only as 'the Operation.'"

"Banal as can be."

"Russ called me a few hours before his supposedly accidental death, all psyched because the Project was closing down and he was going to meet with some NRO people that night about making his felony go away. Coincidentally, I found regular 'grants' in the Septimus Foundation's books to 'the Operation.' I don't know when they started–I only went back to the first of the year–but they stopped right around the time Russ drowned."

Donny was building a very thin circumstantial case. Normally Hari would delight in shooting something like this down in flames, but the pain in his eyes stopped her. He was hurting for his brother.

But he seemed to have left out one major point that she couldn't let pass.

"Motive?"

"Isn't it obvious?"

"Not to me."

"Okay. Follow my logic: Shorting the Internet stocks shows that Septimus knew the crash was coming; most likely they were intimately involved in making it happen since in all Art's research he couldn't find anyone else making similar bets. In order to wreck the Net, they posed as the NRO and hired a bunch of hackers from the dark web to perfect intrusion software. When the work was done, they had to eliminate them because they'd recognize their own work in the worms and trojans that helped bring down the Net."

It made a queer sort of sense, but...

"Again: motive? You've given a motive for killing your brother, but not for bringing down the Net. I can't buy that they'd go all through that just to clean up on the crash."

"We may never know the real reason, but the fact remains that they *did* clean up. And instead of reinvesting that money, they're cashing out. So Art's big question remains: What *else* do they know?"

Hari tapped her fingers on the counter top as she stared at the two dark monitors.

Finally, she said, "We've got work to do."

"Damn right. How do we divide it up?"

"I've got an idea..."

2

Hari worked out a system whereby she would ferret out the dates of large expenditures and Donny would match them with emails–both the deleted and undeleted kind–in and around the same date.

The deleted emails turned out to be the key. The foundation obviously didn't want to leave a record of its cash investments, so it used deposits to and from intermediary banks to hide the transactions. But the deleted emails gave it all away when they mentioned the purchase target by name.

"So they bought Sirocco Trucking in Albany," Hari said. "That was the last thing I would have expected."

"Yeah." Donny swiveled his chair back and forth. "Why a trucking company of all things?"

"Obviously they're planning on shipping something–lots of something."

"But what?"

"The 'what' will probably answer Art's question. Keep looking."

Hours later they'd determined only that the foundation had bought a distributor, but a distributor of what remained a mystery. Without a name, or address they remained in the dark.

"At least we know the trucking company," Hari said finally. Her eyes burned from staring at the screen. "I don't think it's a stretch to say that whatever they're shipping, its source will be their distributor."

Donny gave her a frustrated look. "Big help."

"After all this research, we're left with two nagging questions: What are they shipping and to where are they shipping it? I can think of only one way to find out."

"What? We've gone through all the emails and spreadsheets. What's left?"

Hari rose and gave a single clap. "Road trip!"

"What? To Albany? That's, like, a hundred-fifty miles."

"It's an hour flight, non-stop. I've done it countless times–United's nine-thirty out of Newark. You've got the credit card. Get us seats for tomorrow morning. We'll have Sirocco Trucking under surveillance by noon."

MONDAY—MAY 15

Ernst

Belgiovene stepped into Ernst Drexler's office at precisely 9 a.m. Ernst appreciated punctuality.

"You have work for me?" he said in a surprisingly deep voice for such a slim man.

He stood five-ten, wafer thin, with a small, blue-black mole in the center of his chin. No one seemed to know or remember his first name, or if he had one. Or if Belgiovene was even his real name. He was simply "Belgiovene," though he insisted on everyone pronouncing the terminal vowel.

"It would seem so," Ernst said. "Someone is threatening to do great damage to the Order. We would like to prevent that."

No need for more specificity than that. Belgiovene would know exactly how Ernst meant for him to prevent that damage. His skill was in making murder look like an accident or suicide.

His smile was as thin as the rest of him. "Only one?"

His last assignment had involved eliminating a group of hackers the Order had assembled to provide unwitting help with the assault on the Internet.

"Only one." Ernst slid a slip of paper across the desk. "He's a writer and here's his address."

The smile broadened as he read it. "Alphabet City. Practically a neighbor."

"Your preventative measures should involve confiscation of whatever computers he might possess–for practical reasons, since they hold the damaging materials, but also to make robbery appear the motive."

Belgiovene gave a little bow. "Consider it done. Any timetable?"

"ASAP. Before he can publish his drek."

"I'm get right on it."

The door had barely closed behind Belgiovene when Slootjes entered.

"I saw Belgiovene," the loremaster said. "Is he...?"

"He's on his way."

Slootjes sighed with relief. "Good. I've been watching Winslow's website and he's made no announcement."

"Perhaps it was all bluster," Ernst said. "I hope I didn't send Belgiovene out for nothing."

Not that it really mattered. Belgiovene enjoyed the work. As a member of the Septimus order's security and enforcement wing, he followed orders. But Ernst was aware that he freelanced on the side.

Slootjes said, "Winslow sounded genuinely angry when he stormed out last night. I wouldn't put self-publishing past him. He–"

A knock on the door and then the acolyte acting as the Lodge's receptionist stuck his head inside.

"Sorry to interrupt, sir, but there's a woman out here insists on seeing you."

Well, she obviously wasn't a member–Septimus didn't accept females–and Ernst had a busy morning ahead of him.

"Put her off."

"I've already tried that but she won't go."

"Then have her bodily removed."

"She says she has a memoir written by her grandfather in which the Order in general, and your grandfather in particular, play a very large part." He gave a shy smile. "That's pretty much a quote."

Ernst froze. "Did she now?" He glanced at Slootjes who gave a quick nod. "Very well, send her in." When the acolyte had disappeared, Ernst turned to the loremaster and saw the same question in his eyes. "Yet *another* manuscript?"

"Let's hope it's not as damaging as last night's."

"It had better not be." He jabbed a finger at Slootjes. "You stay right where you are. This might concern you as well."

"A memoir about your grandfather, the famous and mysterious Rudolph Drexler?" The loremaster smiled. "Oh, you couldn't get me out of here with a pry bar."

The acolyte admitted a rather plump woman who looked to be about sixty or so. Her gray hair was wound up in a bun at the back of her head. She wore a simple dress with long sleeves. She might have been Amish except for that fact that she was bareheaded. She had a large shoulder bag from which a fat manila envelope protruded.

"Grace Novak," she said, striding in and extending her hand. "You must be Mister Drexler. I was told you wear a white suit year-round."

"Oh, and who told you that?"

"I made enquiries about you. That's how I traced you here."

Ernst made a quick introduction of Slootjes, then...

"What is this about a memoir, Mrs. Novak?"

"You can call me Grace. I'll make this quick. My mother died recently–"

"My condolences," Slootjes said. Ernst didn't bother.

"She was the only daughter of a man named Charles Atkinson who left this memoir of his years working with Nikola Tesla in the early nineteen hundreds. She in turn left it to me."

She placed the envelope on Ernst's desk. As she rattled on, Slootjes picked it up and removed a thick sheaf of papers from within.

"In it he talks about Tesla's wireless experiments with his tower at Wardenclyffe out on Long Island and how your Septimus order funded him after J.P. Morgan backed out. He also says the funding was overseen by a Septimus member named Rudolph Drexler who, I gather, was your grandfather."

"You gather correctly, Mrs. Novak. But what–?"

"This is heavily redacted in certain sections," said Slootjes who'd been flipping through the pages as the woman was speaking.

"Yes. My mother took a black marker to areas she said were 'too personal.'"

Too personal...interesting.

Ernst's grandfather had disappeared in 1906 and was never seen again. The archives contained photos of Rudolph Drexler taken just across the hall from Ernst's office, posing with the remains of the chew wasps he had killed at Wardenclyffe in the spring of 1904. A dashing figure, grinning as he casually cradled the broomhandle Mauser he'd used to shoot them out of the air. The chew wasps eventually had rotted to dust, but the photos remained. Ernst was sure Slootjes could locate them on a moment's notice.

Two years later his grandfather vanished without a trace. His car and his silver-headed cane–the very same cane Ernst carried every day–had been found parked in the alley behind this building. His fate had long been one of the Order's great ongoing mysteries.

"What do you want for this?" Slootjes said.

She blinked in surprise. "Want for what? The memoir? I'm not–"

"Well, you came here to sell it, didn't you?"

She looked offended. "Not at all. I just thought Mister Drexler would want to learn a piece of his family history that he could not possibly obtain from any other source." She smiled. "My grandfather talking about your grandfather...it seems only right that you should have a copy, don't you think?"

The loremaster's expression and posture radiated skepticism. "You're *giving* it to us?"

"Of course. As I said, it's a copy. The original's back in Schaumburg. I'm here sightseeing with my husband and thought I'd use the opportunity to drop it off."

Ernst pointed to the manuscript. "Does it reveal my grandfather's fate?"

Her expression became uncertain. "I'm not...I'm not sure."

"Oh? I'd assumed you've read it."

"I have, but I'm not sure I believe it."

An uneasy feeling began seeping through Ernst. "What do you mean?"

"It's rather fantastic. But before you read it, I want you to understand something very important: My grandfather was an electrical engineer–a logical man, a practical man, and an honorable one. He was brutally honest about himself in that memoir–the redacted parts–so I cannot conceive of him fabricating other parts. If he wrote it, then he believed it to be the truth."

"Then what is the problem?" Ernst said.

"As I said, I'm sure he believed what he wrote, but some of it is simply not believable to me...not believable in a sense that I don't see how it can be true. But if it *is* true..." Her expression turned bleak. "Then this world is not what we think it is."

No one spoke for a few heartbeats until Slootjes said, "This is very generous of you, Grace. We will study it and store it safely in our archives."

Ernst found his voice. "What...what happened to my grandfather?"

"It's not clear, exactly," she said, shaking her head. "You wouldn't believe me if I told you, so I think it's best you read it yourself. Good day, gentlemen."

Without another word or a backward glance, she turned and scooted from the office.

After a long pause, Slootjes said, "Do you want me to review it first?"

Ernst could tell that the loremaster wanted nothing more in the world than just that. And Ernst had to admit that he wanted to grab the manuscript himself, shove Slootjes out the door, and pore over it. But his schedule was packed–so much going on all over the region– and he knew he wouldn't be able to bestow the kind of attention it deserved.

"Yes. Do that. And while you're at it, do some vetting of whatever facts you find. See if it's worth my time or just the fever dream of some demented old *Kauz*."

"Yes-yes!" Slootjes said as he hurried out. "Absolutely!"

Alone finally, Ernst stepped to the window and stared out at the busy street, full of people going about their everyday lives, completely unaware that the Change was imminent. And yet now, on the verge of the apocalypse, was he about to learn his grandfather's fate? Were they somehow linked?

Mrs. Novak's words echoed through his brain: *You wouldn't believe me if I told you, so I think it's best you read it yourself...*

Her ominous tone and bleak expression as she'd spoken those words had left Ernst with an unsettled feeling.

Barbara

"Whoa!" Bess said when she saw what Ellie had been building. "Looks like we've got a budding Gaudi here."

I have to confess I didn't know what she was talking about. I knew she'd been taking artsy courses so I assumed he was a sculptor of weirdly shaped objects, because Ellie's construction was very weird. Disturbingly so.

I'd called Bess last night and told her not to go to the hospital because Ellie was already gone. So she'd arrived at the apartment where we watched Ellie begin her "shelter." She'd barely spoken while she worked at attaching her found objects to the wall, so Bess finally returned to her dorm.

Normally I wouldn't let one of my daughters get away with that sort of rude behavior, but Ellie was not herself. Nor was I, not really. She'd been through a horrible ordeal and I wasn't about to start an argument. For the time being she had carte blanche.

On the way home from the hospital we'd made a couple of stops to pick up the hammer, nails, screws, drill, glue, soldering iron, and protractor she claimed she needed. I'd been too happy to see her up and about to argue or question, I just paid for it all.

As soon as we reached the apartment she went to work, attaching her junk to the wall. I could see the wall was going to need a lot of repairs to bring it back to its original state but, again, I didn't argue or protest. Anyway, she seemed so driven, I didn't think I'd have any influence.

When she ran out of junk, she'd go out searching for more. I'd trail along because I was afraid of letting her out alone at night. Midtown was pretty safe, but she was a distracted teenage girl, not exactly tuned in to her surroundings. My presence worked out to her advantage though, because she used me as a pack mule.

Wood, metal, plastic straws, Styrofoam, flattened aluminum cans, paper towel tubes, doweling, wire coat hangers, pens, pencils, the broken neck of an old guitar, anything that caught her eye. Then back to the apartment again to affix it to her construction.

We did this all night, back and forth, in and out. At times she had me help her–hold something just so while she glued or screwed or soldered it in place. I'd started off thinking this was just some hodgepodge conglomeration of junk–one of those "street art" constructions that found their way into museums now and then.

"Do you have any idea about what this is going to look like when you're through?" I asked her when it had reached halfway up the wall.

"I don't have just 'any' idea, Mother, I have an *exact* idea about what it's going to look like–what it *must* look like when I'm through."

I didn't see how that was possible, considering the random way she seemed to be throwing all the trash together. Well, it looked random, but as it grew, and as I saw how precise she was with the placement of her pieces of junk, I began to think she might have a plan. When she had me hold a piece in place while she affixed it to the whole, I had to hold it *just so*. Many times she'd use a protractor to get an angle exactly right.

Gradually, as we worked through the night–sleep was not an option–it began to take shape. Exactly what sort of shape I'm not sure, but a shape of some sort. In the base was an arched opening, maybe two feet high and two-and-a-half feet wide, but only a foot deep where it dead-ended at the outer wall of her room. If Ellie was constructing this to be a "shelter"–whatever that was supposed to mean–I could see no way she'd fit in there.

At sunrise she was still at it, though running out of trash. Only a few random pieces left. I was drained and sleep deprived and prayed she wouldn't want to make another foraging trip.

Maybe she sensed my exhaustion.

"Almost finished, Mother. Just these last pieces to fix in place and I'll be done. But they've got to go in exactly the right spot at exactly the right angle, so bear with me."

...in exactly the right spot at exactly the right angle...

She had to be joking. The shelter, the construction, the *thing* was a totally random, asymmetrical, eight-foot pile of junk stretching from floor to ceiling. Further proof that this was no longer my Ellie. My Ellie wouldn't make something like this. My Ellie liked order, not chaos. This was pure chaos.

I slumped on the bed and watched her standing on a chair while she worked with her protractor on those last pieces.

*Almost finished...*then what?

I decided to ask: "So Ellie, what are you going to do with this when you finish it?"

Her response came out garbled because she had her protractor clamped between her teeth while she held something in place, but it sounded like she was going to take shelter.

"Shelter from what?"

Garbled again, but I thought she said so she could be by herself.

I looked askance at the little arched space at floor level and said, "But how are you going to be-?"

And just then Bess rang from the downstairs vestibule and I buzzed her in. When she arrived she froze in the doorway to Ellie's room. She hovered there and stared for what seemed like a long time, then stepped inside, still staring.

She made that Gaudi remark, then said, "No, not Gaudi, more like *objet trouvé.*"

"Could you speak English?" I said, more sharply that I intended. I was so *tired.*

Bess seemed not to notice. She kept staring. "It means 'found object'-it's an art form. Yo, Sis. Where'd you ever learn to do something like this?"

"In my coma," Ellie said, still standing on the chair. "I learned that the angles have to be just right. I learned a lot in my coma. Like how to heal my burns and how to build a shelter, and all about what's coming."

"Heal your burns?" I said. "What does that mean?"

Instead of answering, Ellie hopped off her chair and pulled it aside, then stepped back to appraise her work, cocking her head this way and that.

"Uh-huh," she said, nodding with satisfaction. "I think I've got it right."

Bess gave a soft laugh. "How on Earth would you know if you got it wrong?"

Bess had a point. Ellie's *objet trouvé* had no symmetry, no rhyme or reason. It crumbled over the arched base, then undulated up the wall, widening here, narrowing there, shooting branches left toward the window, then right toward the room's corner, back and forth until it stopped at the ceiling.

"We'll know in a few minutes," Ellie said.

As I tried to fathom what she meant, I noticed a tube of glue on the bed. I didn't want it to leak on the spread, so I bent to pick it up... and as I did–

One of the branches disappeared.

I gave a little gasp and straightened, and suddenly the branch was there again.

"You okay, Mom?" Bess said.

I didn't reply. Instead, keeping my eye on the branch, I bent again and...slowly it faded from view.

"Oh, dear God! Something's wrong with that thing!"

Bess stepped to my side.

"What do you–holy shit!" Obviously she'd seen it too. She stepped back. "Ohmigod, the whole top just disappeared. Ellie, do you see this?"

"Uh, huh. It's all a matter of getting the geometry just right."

Bess moved again. "Now the top's back but the whole left side is gone! Ellie, what the *fuck*!"

"Bess!" I said, but I knew how she felt. What the fuck indeed.

"Nothing's actually gone," Ellie said, keeping her eyes fixed on the lower part of the construction. "It simply angles into another place."

"'Another place'?" Bess's eyes were wide. "What does that even *mean*? Another plane of existence, another dimension, the other side of the wall, *what*?"

Ellie shrugged. "Yeah, I guess so. Sort of."

"'Sort of'? Wh-wh-wh-wh–" Bess sounded like a stuck record.

And then I felt a warm breeze against my shins. It flowed from under the bed. No, it came from the pile, from the arch at its base, and flowed under the bed.

And the arch...the opening was dark now. Where I used to be able to see the floor molding and some of the bedroom wall...only blackness now.

"Oh, excellent!" Ellie said. "I did get it right."

Get *what* right? I wanted to say, but couldn't take my eyes off that dark space.

Ellie dropped to her hands and knees. "Okay, I'm going in."

"Going in where?" Bess said with a laugh. "There's no place to go."

"Sure there is. See you later."

With that she crawled through the arch and disappeared inside. "Ellie!" I cried. "Ellie, don't."

Her voice, strangely distorted, echoed back about being by herself.

Bess wasn't laughing anymore. "That's impossible! Mom, she can't–don't let her go!" She dropped to her knees beside the arch and reached inside to grab Ellie's foot or leg but came away with nothing. "Mom, she's gone! But she can't be gone! It's not possible!"

My brain was numb but I knew what she meant.

Ellie's construction lay against an outside wall. A hole in the wall could lead only to empty outside air. Yet Ellie had crawled all the way through and beyond. I rushed to the window and looked out. The outer wall was unmarred. Nothing extended beyond it.

I dropped beside Bess and stuck my head inside. Warm, odorless air flowed against my face.

"Ellie? Ellie! You come back here! You come back here this instant!"

Faintly, as if from a great distance, I heard, "...fine...little while... myself."

Bess fumbled with her key chain and came up with a pen light. Aimed through the arch, its bright beam lit up a long, narrow passage with rippled-ribbed walls of gleaming black. Bright as it was, the beam didn't reach the end.

"Oh, God," I said, and it came out a moan. "This isn't right, it isn't possible."

I so wanted it to be an optical illusion, but I could feel the air flow, so I knew I wasn't just seeing things.

"Mom," Bess said, "we can't both be in the same nightmare, can we? I mean, this stuff doesn't happen in real–"

"I'm going in," I said, but Bess pulled me back as I started to crawl forward.

"Are you crazy? With your back?"

"I can't leave her in there!"

"She *wants* to be in there."

"She says she wants to be by herself but I've got to know if she's all right."

"What if your back goes out?"

"It won't go out."

"But you know what happens when it does. You'll be stuck."

I knew she was right, but...

"That's Ellie in there, Bess. Your little sister. My little girl. I can't just let her disappear into God knows where!"

She did her patented eye roll. "All right, *I'll* go in, okay?"

I could tell she was afraid–who wouldn't be?–but she'd never admit it. She might aspire to a bohemian life but she'd grown up with that Midwestern hold-my-beer approach to challenges.

With her penlight pointed ahead of her, Bess crawled through the arch on her elbows and knees and disappeared into the tunnel. I crouched at the opening and watched her slowly dwindling silhouette. I estimated she was about fifty feet away when she stopped.

Faintly I heard Ellie's voice say, "Hello, Bess," followed by Bess's scream. And then Bess was frantically crawling backward on her hands and knees, making terrified, high-pitched mewling noises as her shoes scrabbled toward me.

I ducked to the side as she emerged, feet and butt first, almost knocking me over. But she didn't stop. She kept up the panicked backward crawl, kept making those terrified noises as she reverse-scuttled across the room until she ran out of floor. It might have been comical were it not for the look of abject horror twisting her face. With her back pressed against the wall, she slid upright, slipped and fell, then regained her feet and stumbled-ran from the bedroom.

I hurried after her and found her at the apartment's front door, her back pressed against it, blinking, cringing, shuddering as she reached for me with a trembling hand.

"M-m-mom!" she panted in a breathless voice. "You've got to get out of here!"

"What's wrong? What happened?"

"You can't stay here! You can crash in my dorm! Lena won't mind!"

"That's crazy talk. I'm not going anywhere while Ellie–"

"That's not Ellie in there!"

Bess had just voiced my greatest suspicion, my worst fear. I felt my knees soften, ready to give way, but I forced them straight and locked them. I wouldn't, *couldn't* acknowledge it.

"Don't be silly. I–"

"I am *not* being silly! You can't stay here!"

"I can and I will and I don't want to hear any more of this. Now come into the kitchen and I'll make you–"

She grabbed the door handle. "No. No way. I can't force you to leave, but me, I'm outa here. You know where my dorm is. You can come any time."

"Bess, please. Get hold of yourself."

She opened the door and slipped through, then turned and looked at me through the narrowing opening.

"You don't get it, Mom. You said she went in there to be by herself. You got it wrong." A sob escaped her. "She went in there to *be* herself."

And then she slammed the door.

I stood there, gaping in shock. Bess...Too-Cool-for-School Bess, the unflappable Boho who took everything in stride...I'd never seen her like this, never imagined she could *be* like this. So terrified...

What had she seen?

My mind reeling, I wandered back to Ellie's bedroom where I stared at the darkness within that low arch. I knew I'd have to go in there.

Frankie

P. Frank Winslow leaned back from his laptop and rubbed his eyes. This self-publishing shit was a lot more involved than he'd thought.

But then, he hadn't really been thinking when he'd threatened to publish *Dark Apocalypse* on his own. He'd been pissed and wanted to shove their lawsuit threats back in their faces. Like he was going to let some glorified Elk's club dictate what he could write about. Were they kidding?

Last night, a corner of his mind had seen himself uploading the Word doc, clicking a *PUBLISH* button, and *voila!*—*Dark Apocalypse* would go on sale under his Phillip F. Winter pseudonym. He hadn't considered the small matter of a cover.

So he'd spent much of the morning searching for an appropriate piece of art and then working it through a cover creator. Those wasted hours were wreaking havoc with his Daily Duty.

He stared at the result on his screen and hated it. He couldn't imagine buying a book with a cover like that, so why should he think anyone else would? Was he actually going to have to *pay* someone good money to create a cover for him? Frankie hated that even more.

Take a break. That was it: Get up, stroll around a bit, then come back with fresh ideas.

Trouble was, his fourth-floor one-bedroom walkup didn't afford much strolling space. The front room doubled as living room and office, furnished with his laptop on the desk, a couch, and a TV. And bookshelves, of course, mostly stocked with copies of his titles.

He made a circuit of the room, then stepped into his little eat-in kitchen and put some water on to boil. A cup of tea would be good about now. From the kitchen he wandered to the sparsely furnished bedroom but stopped inside the door as a breeze wafted against his face.

Where was *that* coming from? He kept his windows closed pretty much all year round. He checked them now–yep, both locked up tight. But still that faint breeze. It seemed to be coming from the rear corner, behind the nightstand.

Years ago, when his mother had downsized, he'd moved his old bedroom furniture from Harrisburg to NYC. The bed was a twin and plenty big enough for him, but the furniture was heavy maple. He'd damn near given himself a hernia moving it all in here, and now he risked one again as he grunted and groaned to angle the nightstand out from the wall for a look.

"Well, I'll be damned."

A section of the floor, maybe three feet in length, appeared to have separated from the side wall. Just a few inches, but if he angled his head right, he could see into the apartment below.

This wasn't good. In fact, this could be very bad. The building dated from the late 1940s, which made it like three-quarters of a century old. It just might be coming apart. He didn't want to be here if it decided to come crashing down.

He understood how he'd missed the gap, hidden away as it was on the floor behind the nightstand. But it opened into the *ceiling* of the apartment below. How had anyone missed that?

He decided to go check.

He didn't know his neighbors much beyond a non-committal nod in the hallways. Didn't really want to. Not because he didn't like them or anything, but he wasn't looking for friends here. He had a few writer friends around the city and they'd get together now and again for drinks and dinner and to bitch about the industry. But truth was he'd actively avoided making friends in the building. He had to bang out a minimum of 2K words every day–what he called his Daily Duty–to keep the royalties flowing and pay the rent.

Frankie took the graffiti-bedizened stairway down to the third floor. Apartment *3F* was directly below his own *4F.* He knocked and waited while he assumed he was being checked out through the peep hole. Then he knocked again.

Finally, a tentative "Who's there?" from the other side.

"Hey, there. I live above you. I think we share some structural damage. Mind if I come in and take a look?"

The door opened and a familiar wrinkled black face peeked out. He recognized her but her name was a blank space in his mind. He'd helped her carry her groceries up the stairs more than a few times.

"I know you," she said in her Jamaican accent. "You that writer mon."

He bowed. "One and the same, ma'am. Look, I won't be a minute but I'd just like to check out your ceiling."

She hesitated, then swung the door open. "I guess I can trust you."

"Seriously"—what the hell was her name?—"I'll be just a sec."

The rooms of her apartment were laid out exactly like his but hers were richly redolent of cooking spices. Jerk chicken, maybe? His mouth watered as he hurried through the front room to the bedroom where—

He stared in shock. The ceiling was perfect.

"Whassa mattah?" she said, coming up behind him.

He stepped closer for a better look. A few minor cracks in the plaster, sure, but no three-inch gap. No gap at all.

How could this be? Was he in the wrong apartment?

He took a mental picture of the bottles and hairbands and such on the dresser right under the spot where the gap should be, then mumbled a lame excuse and hurried upstairs.

Back in his apartment he made a beeline for his bedroom and dragged the nightstand a little farther from the wall—just enough for him to squeeze in behind it for a better look below. Good thing he was skinny. He knelt and craned his neck, but as he leaned on the edge he felt it soften—not crumble but *soften* and—

"Oh, Christ!"

—he tumbled through.

He managed to swing his legs under him and land partially on his feet in a crouch, then plopped onto his butt, damaging nothing beyond his pride. As he straightened he looked around and saw a king-size bed and a dresser against the wall, but its top was bare and made of a different wood from the old Jamaican woman's. He'd landed in someone else's apartment.

Whose then? Not some trigger-happy drug dealer with an AK-47, he hoped. Best to announce himself to avoid surprises. That gap in the corner of the ceiling showed where he'd come through. He could explain everything.

"Hello?" he called, moving toward the door. "Hello?"

No reply, so he peeked out into the short hall leading to the front room. Empty. And the front room looked empty too.

Yes!

One more try: "Hello?"

Again, no answer. He had the place to himself. Okay. Not a good idea to exit by the door–someone might see him and think he was up to no good. Best to go back the way he'd arrived.

In the bedroom he dragged the dresser–luckily it didn't weigh much–under the opening, then placed a chair atop it. Now all he had to do was stretch and haul himself back into his own place. As soon as he was home, he'd get on the line to the property manager.

He pushed his head and chest above the floor line and was straining to lever the rest of himself up when he heard a sound in his living room. He froze and listened.

His apartment door had just opened, and now it closed. Softly.

He opened his mouth to call out but then shut it. He'd locked the door–a reflex when you lived in a place like this–which meant the intruder either had a key or had picked the lock. Frankie had never given a key to anyone.

Shit. Someone was boosting his place.

What would Jake Fixx do?

Well, fuck that. His recurring character–written under his own name–was an ex SEAL who could take down multiple attackers with ease. And what was he? A sedentary writer with atrophied muscles who hadn't worked out since his teens.

He'd wait it out and hope he wasn't discovered.

But the big question was *why*–why would anyone break into his place? He had no valuables beyond his laptop, which wasn't particularly high end anyway. And even if that were stolen, all his work was backed up in Dropbox. So who–?

Wait. The Septimus folks? Could it be?

He'd been thinking of them as some sort of stuck-up BPOE group, but at the meeting last night the two honchos there had said the Octogon Brotherhood in Frankie's book was too much like Septimus for comfort. The Octogon had come to him in one of his dreams–utterly ruthless, eliminating anyone who got in its way like the average Joe would swat a fly. And those Septimus honchos had made it very clear they did *not* want *Dark Apocalypse* published.

Had they sent someone to make sure that didn't happen? Ever?

This was the kind of stuff he wrote about. *Fiction.* It didn't happen in real life–at least not to him.

Frankie held his breath as the intruder stomped into his bedroom. He watched the guy's Nikes through the one-inch gap between the rug and the bottom of the nightstand. Saw him get down on his hands and knees and check under the bed.

Please don't look back here! *Please*, don't look back here!

He didn't. Frankie released his breath when the guy stormed out of the room.

What to do? He couldn't stay here, balancing on a chair set atop a dresser. His best bet was to–

Out in the front room, the intruder started to talk to someone. Were there *two* of them?

"Hey, it's Belgiovene. I'm in the guy's apartment but he's not around…yeah, his laptop's here, open and running, so I don't think he'll be out long."

Sounded like he was on a phone.

"Well, in a way this works out better. I'll lock his door just like he left it and be waiting for him when he wanders back in…right, won't know what hit him…and yeah-yeah, I know: Take the laptop." A pause, then a muttered, "Fuck you, Drexler. This ain't my first rodeo."

The realization that this guy was here to either kill him or beat the crap out of him almost tumbled Frankie off the chair. Time to retreat. Bending his shaky knees and praying he didn't lose his balance, he lowered himself to the dresser and then to the floor.

Okay. No heroics. Call the cops and report a thief or a home invader or whatever in his apartment. He pulled out his phone, punched in 9-1-1, and waited. When no one answered, he repeated. Then he noticed *No Service* on the screen. How could that be? The only place in this city with no service was a deep basement or a subway tunnel without a repeater.

He stepped into the kitchen and grabbed the wall phone there but got no dial tone. And what the fuck–a *rotary* phone?

Had to find a spot with a signal.

He hurried out to the hall but stopped when he reached it. None of this looked familiar. And the number on the apartment door said *11-M*. No way. He'd come down to the third floor, right below his own place.

Feeling like reality was slipping away, he hit the stairs and stopped again. What happened to all the graffiti? The stairwell had been coated with bullshit tags. This one was clean–totally clean.

Shaky now, he hurried up to the next floor–supposed to be the fourth but the door was labeled *12*.

What's going *on?*

He peeked down the hall. His was the fifth door down and it stood open. In fact, all the apartment doors were open.

And then the silence hit him. He realized he hadn't heard a human voice or a single note of music since he'd left *11-M.* That just didn't happen in his building. Some asshole was always blasting rap or salsa or something equally obnoxious behind one of the doors.

Where is everybody?

Frankie crept down the hall and peeked into his own place.

Except it wasn't his place. The furniture wasn't the same, the walls were a different color, no work desk, no laptop, no bookshelves, and…and the emptiness was palpable. The whole *building* felt deserted.

He stepped to the nearest window where he looked out on a city he'd never seen before. He didn't know where he was but that wasn't the Lower East Side out there. Nothing on the skyline looked familiar. And worse–nothing was moving–empty streets, empty sidewalks. The place looked like a ghost town.

"Shit!"

Before he knew it he was fleeing along the hall and down the stairs and back to *11-M.* He'd take his chances with Belgiovene or whatever he called himself. At least he'd be back in New York, not this…this empty movie set.

He charged into the bedroom and began to climb onto the dresser when he noticed that the ceiling was intact. No gap. Not even a crack. Sealed up as if nothing had ever been wrong.

Frankie kneeled on the chair and pounded on the ceiling where the gap had been.

"No! *NO!*"

Hari

The propjet flight from Newark was noisy and bumpy but on time. Enterprise had their rental–a black Taurus–ready and waiting, the only hitch being a brief argument over who would drive, which Donny lost. Hari didn't like being a passenger, so she convinced Donny he'd be the better navigator. Once they got rolling they had a second argument when Donny wanted to play music from his phone through the car's sound system. Thirty seconds' worth was all she could stand.

"I would call that bad music," she said, turning it off, "but that would classify it as music, which it most definitely is not."

"You don't like DMX? He's from my high school days."

"He makes the B-52s sound good."

"Who are the B-52s?"

"You never heard of–I don't believe it. 'Rock Lobster?' The worst rock song ever?"

A head shake. "Nope. Sorry."

"Don't be sorry. Consider yourself lucky. Find a country station."

He looked horrified. "Country? You like *country*?"

She didn't, but she figured he'd like it less.

By noon they were cruising through an industrial park just outside Albany where Sirocco Trucking occupied a huge warehouse. Hari passed it once to get the lay of the land. It sat on a low rise with a big, tree-lined parking lot. Good thing she had the address because no one had bothered to put a sign out front, just a number.

She swung back and turned into a gently curving driveway. She found a space in the packed parking lot and spotted a uniformed guard walking a German shepherd. She didn't like the way the dog tugged toward their car, so she called from her window.

"Excuse me! This is Sirocco Trucking, right?"

He approached with the dog and stopped a dozen feet away. His dark blue uniform housed a running back's build that had yet to go to seed. His baseball cap with its Septimus Security logo, his big aviator sunglasses, and his thick mustache didn't leave much of his face visible, but what Hari could see looked surprised.

"You're looking for Sirocco? Well, I guess you found it."

She guessed they didn't get many drop-ins.

"Great. Where's the office?"

"The office…the office is around the corner but no one's there."

"Out to lunch?"

"No one's ever there. Can I help you?"

Damn. They'd been assuming they could at least get inside the building.

"We'd like to rent a truck."

"They don't rent trucks."

During this scintillating repartee, another guard in identical garb with an identical dog rounded a corner and stopped to watch.

What *is* this? Hari thought. Do we somehow look threatening?

"I mean," she said, "we'd like to arrange to ship some things."

"All their trucks are spoken for."

"*All* of them?"

"Every one."

He sounded coached.

"Do you think we might have a look at them?"

"That's not an option, ma'am."

"Are you sure?" she said. "Is there someone I can speak–?"

"The office is empty and I'm afraid you can't park here."

Hari gave him a hard stare. He stared back through his shades.

And that was all she wrote. Hari could see she wasn't going to win here, so she backed out of her space and headed down the drive.

"That went well," Donny said. "What now?"

"Notice anything?" she said as they hit the industrial park's common boulevard.

"Besides guys patrolling the grounds of a trucking company with dogs? I mean, seriously–German shepherds? Whoever heard of that? It tells me they're majorly paranoid about someone glomming onto whatever it is they're up to. And as for little boy blue back there, he wasn't giving anything away. I mean, nada."

"All good points. But I'm more interested in the parking lot."

A pause, then, "Full. *Lots* of cars." Another pause as he rubbed his stubble. "They could belong to drivers arriving to take a haul somewhere."

"Exactly. The question is: Have they already left, or are they gathering to leave together?"

Donny grinned. "A convoy? Seems unlikely, but only one way to find out. I see a stake-out in our future. Let's get some food first. We need to stock up on munchies. I saw a strip mall back by the highway with some fast-food joints."

Hari knew where he meant and headed there.

"Speaking of fast food," she said, "did you hear how McDonald's bought the Wendy's logo and won't let them use it? So pretty soon, unless you already know where your Wendy's is, you won't be able to find one."

"You're kidding!"

"Yep."

A long pause, then a sigh, then, "Y'know, one day that mouth of yours could get you killed."

"I know. Can't wait."

At the mall Hari picked up two large coffees–both for her–at an espresso bar while Donny bought these box lunches from Taco Bell that contained enormous amounts of food. Then they found a parking spot in the lot of the FedEx depot across the boulevard with a view of the Sirocco driveway.

"Do you ever drink anything that doesn't contain caffeine?" Donny said just before cramming a soft taco into his face.

"Only when forced by circumstance. You don't want to know me when I run low."

The wait turned out to be shorter than Hari had anticipated. In fact she'd expected to be watching trucks returning from a haul. But at 1:22 one tractor-trailer after another started pulling out and heading for the freeway. Half of the trailers were rectangular freight semis, while the rest were tankers.

Hari counted ten rigs in all. When it looked like no more were joining the parade, she pulled out and followed.

"Odd time for a convoy, don't you think?" Donny said. "I mean, if you're not keen on drawing attention, an afternoon truck convoy is not the way to go."

"Makes even less sense when you consider the level of security they have around the building. I'd give anything for a look inside one of those trailers. Just a peek. Then we can head back."

Maybe they'd all pull into a rest stop and she could sneak up on one.

"What about those tankers? They could be filled with anything–gasoline, water, chemicals, slime, *anything*."

"'Slime'?"

"Yeah. Green goop. I'm guessing you never watched Nick."

"Who's he?"

"It's a cable channel. Nickelodeon."

As Donny launched into an explanation she only half heard, Hari followed the convoy to 787 North where it rolled to Troy, then crossed the Hudson onto Route 2 East.

"Where the hell are we going?" she said.

The car came equipped with its own wi-fi hotspot and Donny had his tablet fired up and running.

"If we stay on Two here, it'll bring us into the Taconic Mountains."

"How long's that going to take?"

"Not bad–forty-five minutes or so to the Massachusetts border."

"And then what?"

"Lots of mountains."

Great. Hari hadn't planned on any of this. She'd expected a few hours' worth of nosing around to yield what they wanted–the nature of the cargo. That, in turn, would lead them to the reason for the Septimus stock sell off.

Route 2 soon started calling itself Taconic Trail, and seemed to be running perpetually uphill. Which meant slow going in the lower gears for the big rigs. They passed the Massachusetts line and kept on trucking.

"How much longer?" Hari groaned.

"Well, since I don't know the destination, I can't very well–"

"Rhetorical! Rhetorical!"

A couple of miles into Massachusetts the trucks took a left off Route 2 onto a narrow side road. A sign with an arrow read *Norum Hill.*

"I think we just learned their destination," Donny said. "Norum Hill."

Hari turned and followed them up the mountain road. "How do you know they're not going to keep on rolling?"

"Because according to the map, this road goes to the summit

where there's some kind of memorial to an Indian chief whose-"

"It's 'Native American,'" Hari said. "*I'm* Indian."

"Right. Sorry. Anyway, I can't pronounce his name, but the road ends there. When you want to come down you have to use this road."

The road could barely fit two cars.

"Not with those trucks on it you're not. How do they-?"

A cop car with *Berkshire County Sheriff* emblazoned on the door was parked on the shoulder ahead. An armed deputy in a tan uniform, Stetson hat, and Sam Brown belt, who had been lounging against the front grille, stepped into the road and held up his hand.

Donny stuck his head out the passenger window. "What's the problem, officer?"

"Rock fall ahead. You need to turn around and go back."

"What about all those trucks we've been stuck behind like forever?"

"They're gonna be a problem." He didn't budge from the middle of the road. "We have to get them turned around somehow. In the meantime, you've got to go back down to the highway and stay off this road."

"But-"

His voice hardened. "We're both speaking English, aren't we? Turn around, go back down to the highway, and stay off this road."

Hari waved at the deputy and began backing up.

"Hey, Hari," Donny said, "what are you doing? We need to-"

She lowered her voice and said, "What we need is to not draw attention to ourselves. Look at Deputy Dog's face. He's not going to let us by."

"But he's lying."

"Of course he is. He might not even be with the sheriff's department. But you said it yourself: This road ends at the summit. What goes up, must come down. We simply have to wait."

They parked farther east on Route 2 where they had a discrete and only partially obstructed view of the turnoff. Hari lowered the windows, turned off the engine, and they settled in to wait.

It turned out to be a short wait-half an hour, tops-before the convoy started rolling back onto the Taconic Trail and heading downhill toward Albany. But only the tractors were rolling. All the semi-trailers had been left behind.

"And there goes Deputy Dog," Hari said as the sheriff's car brought up the rear.

"Why do you keep calling him that?"

"The cartoon. You don't remember *Deputy Dog*?"

"Nope."

"Not important."

Hey, Nineteen started playing in her head.

Hari waited until the sheriff's unit drove out of sight and they had the road to themselves, then headed back up Norum Hill.

"They left their loads up there," Donny said, staring at his tablet.

"Yes, Captain Obvious."

"But where? There's one road to the top with no turnoffs."

He was getting on her nerves.

"Maybe they've created a turnoff that's not on the map. Maybe they left the trailers at the summit."

"Ten semis and tankers?"

"Exactly. You can't hide all those, so can we stop speculating? We're on our way up the mountain. We will see wherever they left them."

But they didn't.

Hari drove all the way to the summit without seeing anything but trees. The top had been flattened somewhat and layered with gravel for parking. A short memorial obelisk stood near a tall cell tower at the northern edge, but otherwise…nothing. The view might have been impressive had Hari's interest in mountain vistas exceeded nil.

Donny got out and inspected the ground.

"No sign of anything with major tonnage up here recently. The gravel would be chewed up."

"Which means we missed it. We'll take it real slow going back down."

But before leaving the summit she did a slow circuit of the perimeter of the groomed area. The Norum Hill road stayed mostly on the eastern and northern faces of the mountain and she saw why. The western face was much steeper.

"See anything that looks like a bunch of trucks down there?" she said.

Donny craned his neck to look but neither of them saw any sign of the trailers.

"Nothing. How is this possible? I've got a topographical map of this place on my tablet and, according to that, the summit here is the only even vaguely flat spot on the whole hill. There's no place that'll accommodate ten semis but here."

"Obviously you're wrong," she said.

"I'm not. I'm..." He ran out of words.

"Think about it: We saw them pull trailers up, we saw them come down without them, so that means the trailers are still up here. We simply have to find them."

Hari took her time on the way back down, and somewhere near the halfway point they spotted a break in the trees that hadn't been apparent on the way up.

"Gotta be it," Donny said.

The road didn't branch here, but two well-worn ruts angled off through the underbrush between trees. Hari hesitated to turn in, unsure about backing out. She pulled onto the shoulder-extra wide here-and parked.

"Let's reconnoiter on foot," she said.

Donny pointed to the pavement as they crossed the road. "Lots of heavy traffic turning here. Gotta be the place."

Hari wasn't so sure. With the cliff face looming above them, she didn't see any place to go. She did see fairly fresh tree stumps that had been sawed off a ground level. Someone had cut a path through here not too long ago.

But to her amazement, the trail ended abruptly at a sheer rock wall.

"This is impossible," Donny cried, slapping his palms against the granite or whatever the hell these mountains were made of. "Look at the tire ruts! They run right up to the rock-*right up to it!* It's as if it was lowered over the trail like a curtain."

A perfect description. The tire ruts didn't stop a foot before the rock face, they didn't stop an inch before it: They stopped against it-as if the rigs had driven straight through solid rock, unhitched their trailers inside the mountain, then driven out again.

The perfect impossibility of that gave her a deep, uneasy feeling. Because it looked like that was exactly what had happened. Which made no sense.

She did a slow turn, looking for an answer. Her world was

numbers, and numbers made sense. They didn't lie. People might try to make them lie, but in the end they always told the truth.

As she completed the turn she noticed with a start that Donny had disappeared. Just like the trailers.

"Donny? Don–?"

"Coming," he said as he trotted up the trail toward her, waving a tire iron.

"What's that for?"

"It's got to be a trick."

He stopped before the stony expanse and hammered at it with the iron. It made just the kind of *clank* one would expect from steel striking solid stone. Moving back and forth he kept striking the stone until finally hurling the tire iron back down the trail with a frustrated howl.

"There's got to be an answer!"

"Of course there is," Hari said. "We just don't know it. Yet. We get back in the car and inspect the road with a fine-tooth comb."

"But the tracks clearly show heavy traffic turning in here."

Hari started back toward the car. "We keep looking."

And look they did, up and down the mountain road, but found nothing. Being on the east side of the hill, they lost the light early and were forced to call it quits.

As they headed back toward Albany, Donny said, "Didn't Sherlock Holmes say something about eliminating the impossibles or the like?"

She knew that one. "You mean, 'When you have eliminated the impossible, whatever remains, however improbable, must be the truth'? That one?"

"That's the one. I feel we've eliminated the *possible*, so that leaves us with *im*possible."

"'Impossible,' by definition cannot be, so what we're really left with is the improbable."

"Sounds like word games, but I'll play. What's the next step?"

"We find a hotel, eat, sleep, and get back to the industrial park first thing in the morning."

"How do we know there'll be another convoy?"

"Did you see the size of that warehouse? I'm guessing they've got a lot of whatever to move and I don't see them wasting any time."

He grinned. "Hotel, huh? How many rooms we renting?"

She had to laugh. "You're kidding, right?"

A wider grin. "Well, one room would save Art some money."

She pointed to the radio. "See if you can find a classic rock station. Maybe they're playing Aerosmith."

"Aero...?" His brow furrowed, then he laughed. "Oh, I get it. *Dream On*, right?"

"Riiiiight."

At least he knew that one. But then, everybody knew Aerosmith.

Barbara

I'm ashamed to admit that it took me a couple of hours to muster the courage to enter the passage. I spent much of the intervening time with my head under the arch, calling to Ellie. Apparently, in her panic, Bess had dropped her penlight and it remained on, lighting the end of the passage with a faint glow.

As for Ellie, early on she answered once with a faint "...busy..." and went silent after that.

Finally, I could put it off no longer. I had to find my daughter. I lowered myself to my hands and knees and, fixing my gaze on the glow ahead, began a slow, careful crawl–careful in that I kept my back slightly arched to prevent it from going into spasm. When that happened, it rendered me useless, sometimes for days.

As I moved I noticed a slight incline. Viewed from the arch, the tunnel had seemed level, but from within it definitely tilted upward. The soft, faintly warm airflow persisted and, as I approached, the glow slowly expanded to illuminate the terminal section of tunnel wall surrounding it, leaking into the chamber beyond.

I slowed. I felt winded. I couldn't see how it could be due to exertion because I walked regularly, so it had to be nerves. After witnessing Bess's reaction, did I really want to see Ellie–the new Ellie– being herself?

I had no choice. I had to push on.

Ellie's voice echoed down the passage. "Is that you, Mother?"

"Y-yes." My mouth had gone dry.

"Don't come in here."

"Why not?"

"I don't think it's a good idea."

"But–"

"I upset Bess. I don't want to upset you."

Upset? Bess had been *horrified*. But...

"You're my daughter. I need to see you. You can't lock yourself away like this."

"It's just for a little while. I've got things to do, and then I'll be out."

But I needed to see her *now*, and I'd come this far, so I pushed ahead. Grabbing Bess's penlight, I crawled into the dark chamber–a round floor about fifteen feet across, with a shadowy domed ceiling maybe ten feet high. I sat back on my haunches and fanned the beam around. A half dozen or so white globes the size of snowballs littered the floor, but no sign of Ellie. Where was she?

"Hello, Mother."

Her voice came from above and so I angled the penlight in that direction...and froze.

Ellie clung to the arching wall about three-quarters of the way up toward the domed center. She clung by long, spindly spider legs that had sprung from her back, slim, many-jointed legs, dark brown, gleaming like mahogany.

With a cry, I dropped the light and crab-scrambled back to the tunnel opening. At least with the beam aimed along the floor, reflecting off those snowballs, I couldn't see her.

"Oh, Ellie!" I cried when I found my voice. "Oh, dear God, *Ellie!*"

"I'm all right, Mother," she said, her voice unsettlingly calm. "Really, I am. And believe it or not, I'm okay with it."

"But what is '*it*'? What's happened to you? Who did this to you?"

"Not so much a 'who' as a 'what.' As for the rest, I don't know. I woke from the coma knowing a lot of things I never knew before, but I don't know why I know them, or why any of this happened. But I sense some sort of purpose."

"How can there be a...?" I heard hysteria creeping into my voice. With a supreme effort I curbed it. "How can there be a purpose to... *this*?"

"It originated from a place with a different set of rules, with a different logic, with different geometries."

I moaned. I felt so bad for her. "I don't understand, Ellie."

"Neither do I, Mother. Not completely. I think causing confusion and fear and grief and dismay is part of it, and yet... I know I shouldn't be okay with it, but somehow I am." A sharp, bitter sound, a harsh imitation of a laugh. "Maybe you should have named me Charlotte instead of Eleanor."

"Charlotte...?" I had no idea what she was talking about.

"My favorite story. You used to read it to me at bedtime."

What was she...? Oh, no.

"*Charlotte's Web*? Oh, Ellie, this is no time for...for..."

"Or remember the time I tried out for the soccer team and they passed on me? Man, if Mister Grellson could see me now."

"Ellie, please!"

How could she joke about this...this horror?

"Just trying to lighten things up, Mother. You know the expression: Sometimes you've got to laugh to keep from crying."

I bit back a sob. Oh, my poor, dear, sweet child.

"Is that what you feel like doing? Crying?"

"A small part of me *is* crying-and screaming and shrieking as well-but it's shrinking, and soon it will be gone."

The old Ellie? Was she talking about the girl she used to be?

Just then another white globe dropped into view and rolled to join the rest. I retrieved the penlight and, drawing a deep, tremulous breath, angled it upward.

Two of Ellie's spider legs were poised before her with a smaller version of one of those white globes trapped between the tips. They were rotating the ball this way and that, forming it out of the silky substance flowing from the tips. As I watched, horridly fascinated, it grew steadily until it matched the others in size, at which point the legs released it to fall to the floor.

"Wh-what are those?"

"I'm not sure."

"Then why are you-?"

"The legs seem to have a mind of their own."

I tried to hold it back, I was trying so hard to be strong for her, but as the legs started spinning another white ball, I couldn't restrain the sob that burst from me.

"Oh, Ellie, why you? Why *you*?"

"I don't know, Mother. Maybe I was the wrong person at the wrong place at the wrong time, but I don't think so."

"What do you mean?"

"Maybe I was destined for this. After all, I've never totally fit in." A small bitter smile. "And now I *really* don't fit in."

True, she'd never taken anything at face value. Questioned everything-*everything*. Her mantra was always *There's something else going on here.*

"The signal is a perfect example," she said.

"Signal? What signal?"

"The noise that almost drove me mad that you and Bess couldn't hear at all."

"It's a signal? Of what?"

"I don't know yet. But I will."

"That man who carried you from the park…he could hear it too."

His words had convinced me that Ellie wasn't having a mental meltdown. In light of what followed, a breakdown would have been far preferable to…this.

"I know," she said. "We who hear the signals are a rare breed. We'll be visiting him soon."

"He told me his name but I don't know where to find him."

"He goes by two names and I have his address."

I shook my head in wonder. "How do you know all this?"

She smiled–a cold grimace. "My coma was very instructive."

The spider legs dropped another globe to the floor.

Ellie said, "Carry as many as you can back to the room, Mother, and stack them on the window sill."

Was I being dismissed? I guessed so.

"Why the window sill?

"You'll like the colors when the sun shines through them."

"But–"

"Mother, please. It will begin in the heavens–soon–so I must be ready."

The globes had a slightly sticky feel and I gathered up as many as I could hold in one arm, then crawled back into the tunnel.

"No matter what you think, Mother," I heard her say behind me, "I'm still Ellie. I know what a good mother you've been, and how patient you've been with me over the years. And I still want my Blanky–not in here, this isn't the place for Blanky, but out there, I'll still need it."

I was sobbing when I reemerged into Ellie's old room, but I managed to arrange the half dozen globes on the window sill as she'd said. Their stickiness proved an asset because they stuck to the glass as well as each other. As I was finishing, another globe rolled from the tunnel and stopped outside the arch. And then another and another. I gathered them up as they arrived and added them to the rising pile that was gradually covering all the window panes.

The sun was high and not hitting the glass, but the window faced west; the setting sun would eventually light up the globes.

You'll like the colors when the sun shines through them...

Would I? I wasn't so sure. In fact I doubted it very much. What did I care about colors? My Ellie, my baby, had been changed into a monster. By whom? Was it because of something she'd done-or *I'd* done?

At least she still wanted Blanky. That part of her lived on.

I bunched it up, buried my face in it, and sobbed.

Ernst

Ernst Drexler returned from his meeting with the Council of Seven and slammed his office door behind him.

Was he being paranoid, or was the Council up to something: planning something, or already running some operation without telling him? He was one of the Order's top actuators, damn it! He should be kept current on all the Order's activities.

Ernst told himself he shouldn't allow these free-form suspicions to distract him, but he couldn't let it go. He'd find out what they were up to and–

A knock and Brother Slootjes entered without waiting to be summoned. They'd known each other long enough to dispense with such formalities.

"Alone?" Slootjes said. "Good."

Ernst recognized the manila envelope cradled in his arm: the memoir from Mrs. Novak. The loremaster looked shaken. That was not good. Ernst's stomach turned.

"So you've read it?"

Slootjes nodded. "I have."

"And?"

"It's quite intriguing, even disturbing, one might say."

Ernst was finding the loremaster's penchant for creating drama more vexing than usual today.

"As disturbing as Winslow's novel? Spit it out, man!"

Slootjes dropped into a chair and looked lost for a few seconds. Then he shook himself.

"If true, it's a shattering document, but I'm a long way from being convinced of its authenticity."

"Did you ever believe it could possibly be true?"

"We both know the Order has its enemies, but I'm finding it hard to imagine them expending this amount of time and effort to perpetrate such an elaborate hoax."

"Details!"

"Very well." He tapped the envelope. "This purports to be the memoir of a British immigrant who graduated MIT in 1903 and went to work for Nikola Tesla at his Wardenclyffe tower. It's common knowledge that J. P. Morgan promised to finance Tesla's broadcast power project, but balked when he realized he would have no way to charge for all the electricity Tesla would be transmitting through the air and the Earth. Atkinson says the Order secretly took over the financing of the tower when Morgan backed out."

"Can you verify that?"

"Probably, but I haven't had time. There's too much else going on in this so-called memoir. According to Atkinson, the tower was successful in transmitting wireless energy, but in doing so it was thinning the Veil, allowing influences and entities to pass from the other side. He states that toward the end he and your grandfather witnessed untold horrors existing on the other side, horrors that would invade our world should the Veil be permanently rent. It says Rudolph realized the Order had been duped into lending a hand in its own destruction. But before he could return to report his findings to the Council, he...he disappeared."

"'Disappeared' how?"

Slootjes's gaze shifted away. "I'd rather you read it yourself. The events grow increasingly disturbing through the course of the narrative and by the end are downright fantastic. I'm not sure I believe it, but the fact remains that no one saw your grandfather leave Wardenclyffe. In fact, he was never seen again."

Silence hung in the air.

Ernst didn't know how to respond to that...his grandfather's unexplained disappearance had been a blow to the Order and even worse for his family. Ernst's father, Ernst the first, had confessed to him of being traumatized, feeling he'd been abandoned by the father he'd worshiped. But since grandfather never surfaced again, despite the Order's best efforts to find him, he was presumed dead, the victim of fatal happenstance or foul play.

But no one had ever mentioned vanishing into thin air.

Finally he cleared his throat. "It *must* be a hoax. That scenario—that we are dupes who are unwittingly bringing about the annihilation of humanity—mimics the propaganda the Enemy's apologists have been spewing for generations."

"Yes, I know," Slootjes said, nodding vigorously, "but the

parallels between this and that fellow Winslow's novel are alarming, to say the least."

"He's a crank."

"Not so this Charles Atkinson. The devil, if you'll pardon the cliché, is in the details, and he gets certain details right. He accurately describes the chew wasps your grandfather put on display here. He even goes so far as to say that after Rudolph disappeared through the Veil, he is the one who drove his touring car back to the city, parking it behind this Lodge with his cane on the seat."

Ernst grabbed the cane from where he always left it leaning against the wall. In 1906 it had been returned to Germany where Rudolph's son, Ernst the first, his father, had still been a boy in his early teens. That Ernst eventually passed it on to his own son. Ernst loved this cane.

"He...he mentions the cane?"

"Absolutely. Describes it right down to the silver head with the Septimus sigil and rhinoceros-hide wrapping. Whoever wrote this either had enough access to our archives to allow him to create a monumental hoax, or..."

"Or it's true?"

Slootjes gave his head a violent shake. "But it *can't* be true. I need to delve into the archives for verifications. I'm sure I can find ample evidence of fakery." He rose and placed the envelope on Ernst's desk. "In the meantime, you read it. You mustn't simply take my word for it. You must read it for yourself while I comb the archives. We can discuss it further tomorrow."

So saying, he made a hurried exit.

Ernst stared at the envelope. He didn't want to read what was inside. Even if it was pure fiction, he didn't want to read about his grandfather, a revered actuator in his time, losing faith with the Order. Nor did he want to read about him disappearing forever.

But Slootjes's description of the memoir's contents echoed his own worst fears: that the Septimus order had been fooled and duped for thousands of years, and that in the end the One would betray them all.

He snatched up the envelope and settled back to read.

Frankie

P. Frank Winslow stared at the mess he'd made of the bedroom.

He'd found a solid steel curtain rod and used it to smash the ceiling plasterboard over the dresser where the gap had existed. Once he'd ripped that away he found himself facing steel-reinforced concrete. No way was he going to get through that, not without a jackhammer.

Where had the gap gone? How could it be open one minute and then gone without a trace the next?

He wanted to scream, he wanted to cry, he wanted to break things. But most of all he wanted a drink–he'd start with water, but after that he'd go for vodka, gin, Scotch, anything. He wasn't going to be choosy.

In the kitchen he filled a glass from the faucet and gulped. *Gah.* Tasted funny. Could water go stale? Maybe a little ice would help. He looked around for the refrigerator and didn't see one.

No fridge? How was that possible? In fact, he didn't see even a space for one. The kitchen had been laid out without a refrigerator. He went through all the drawers and cabinets and found glassware and dishes and utensils, but no canned goods or edibles of any sort except packets of thick crackers.

He unwrapped one of those and inspected it. Looked okay. No mold or anything like that. He bit into it. Damn. Like rock. He tried again and broke off a chunk. It tasted like...like nothing, really. A hint of salt but otherwise he might have been munching on a chunk of that broken plasterboard from the bedroom ceiling. So damn hard–

Wait. He'd done some research for a time-travel story he'd written that involved going back to the Civil War. This stuff was just like what soldiers ate back then–*hardtack*. Keep the crackers dry and they lasted forever. The soldiers use to soak them in water to soften them up and make them more edible. Hardtack was also what they fed prisoners back then.

Was that what this place, this town, this city was–a prison? But if so, where were the prisoners?

None of this made any sense.

He put the big questions aside. He'd figure them out later. Right now he had to master his immediate environment.

Even though he wasn't hungry, which was odd because his usual routine was to graze all day, he knew he needed sustenance. He put a few crackers in a bowl and covered them with some of the stale water. While they were soaking, he figured he'd check out the apartment above again, the one that had been his in another time and place.

Going up, he marveled once more at the graffiti-free stairwell. Back in the apartment bedroom, the floor near the corner remained perfectly intact.

He wandered back to the front room. What was he going to do? How did he get back to his own reality?

He'd seen an elevator door down the hall. He checked and found it working. He hit the button marked L and the car headed down. A button below L was marked B but wouldn't light. It had a keyhole next to it so maybe it needed to be unlocked before it worked.

The elevator let him out in some sort of lobby. Small. A couple of easy chairs and an empty reception counter. He spotted a door to a lighted office behind it but found it deserted. Filing cabinets and a desk sporting an old-fashioned mechanical typewriter, but no human. He checked the filing cabinets—empty.

His gaze wandered to the mechanical typewriter. Not even electric—totally manual. He pulled open a drawer in the desk and found a thick ring of keys, which probably opened every apartment. Another drawer contained a stack of typing paper. He stared at the paper a long time.

Well, why the hell not? He hadn't written a single word all day and missing his Daily Duty was adding to his jumpiness.

Well, "Daily Duty" was what he called it in public. In private he called it "the Disease," because that was what it was. P. Frank Winslow couldn't *not* write. When he wasn't actually putting words on the screen, he was thinking about the words he was going to put on the screen next time he sat down. He'd mentioned it to a doctor once who called it a form of Obsessive-Compulsive Disorder. Always thinking about writing was the obsessive part; his inability to stay away from the keyboard was the compulsive component. The doc said OCD was treatable.

But Frankie couldn't afford treatment. Oh, he could afford the pills, but treating the OCD might very well drop his word count. Many times he found he couldn't stop and he'd go past the 2,000-word target–often enough to bring his annual word count to somewhere in the neighborhood of a million.

A million words sounded like a lot, and it was, and he divided them up between his pseudonyms–thrillers under his own name, horror-SF as Phillip F. Winter, and paranormal romance as Phyllis Winstead. But after his agent and the taxman took their cuts, and he helped pay for his mother's assisted living back in Pennsy, all he could afford in the city was that crummy walk-up on Avenue D that now he missed so much. Yeah, he could have shared a place with someone, or found nicer digs in the outer boroughs, but both of those choices were anathema. P. Frank Winslow lived and worked alone, and NYC was the only place to do it.

He prided himself on having no illusions and no literary aspirations. Not these days, anyway. Starting out, he'd planned to make a big splash in the literary world, but decided to hone his writing chops in genre fiction first. He found it came naturally, and he made money at it, so he kept writing the stuff. It got to the point where he couldn't afford to take off the extended time he'd need to write that big serious novel–the bills arriving every month wouldn't want to hear about it.

He doubted now that he'd ever really had the capacity to explain the human condition. Hell, how could he explain something that had always baffled him? So instead he'd settled on simply trying to make the reader turn the page. He figured he was destined from the start to write pulp, and so he accepted his fate. His target became the gut, not the intellect. He was pressing readers' buttons to trigger visceral responses, and he was good at it. If readers felt like they'd been on an emotional rollercoaster after finishing one of his novels, cool: job well done.

And as for the old *Where do you get your ideas?* question, he had a simple answer: dreams. His subconscious had a seemingly endless reserve of stories it told him while he slept, which he transcribed into novels while awake.

He needed to write and realized he could write about all this, adapt what had been happening to him. Make a sci-fi story out of it. Trapped in a deserted prison city in an alternate universe.

Yeah.

Just a few pages...just to take the edge off...

But he had to figure out how to use this damn typewriter first.

Barbara

Well, Ellie had been right. The sunlight shining through those white globes created a spectacular display.

The globes had rolled out of the passage at a steady pace and I dutifully stacked them one by one against the window until all the panes were covered. They must have numbered about a hundred by then.

I spent the rest of the day wandering aimlessly from room to room. I knew I should eat to keep up strength but my churning stomach rebelled at the thought of taking a single bite. I called Bess to see how she was doing but she still sounded borderline hysterical and kept insisting I leave Ellie and stay with her. But I couldn't do that. I may have dozed off in a chair at some point–I'd been up all night, after all–but I wasn't keeping track of time so I couldn't be sure.

And then the light of the setting sun had reached the window and lit up the globes, changing their color from white to every shade imaginable, painting the opposing wall with a magical light show. An old rock album my father used to play–he never threw out his scratchy vinyl LPs–had a psychedelic song with lyrics about a valley of trees with prism leaves that broke the light into colors "that no one knows the names of." Bad English on their part but it perfectly described what I was seeing. Some of the colors splashing on that wall were like no hue I'd ever imagined. I'd never taken LSD, but I wondered if someone on an acid trip might experience colors like these.

Finally the sun set and the light show faded.

I wandered to the kitchen where I heated up a can of chicken noodle soup and forced myself to eat.

Night had fallen by the time I returned to Ellie's room, but a street light shining outside was now illuminating the globes from below, creating intricate designs on the wall and ceiling. As I gazed at the patterns, I noticed an odd stippling. I stepped to the window for a closer look at the globes themselves and saw that they'd developed finely speckled defects in their cores. An effect from the sunlight?

Finally, I could take the silence no longer. I dropped to my hands and knees and crawled a short way into the passage. I hadn't brought the penlight and inky blackness stretched before me.

"It's me, Ellie," I called.

Her voice echoed back. "I know."

"I'm not coming in, I just wanted to check on how you're doing."

"I'm fine, Mother."

"Are you ever coming out?"

"I'll be ready to leave day after tomorrow."

"Day after-? Why so long?"

"Certain things can't be rushed, Mother. But we'll go out for a nice walk then."

A walk? Looking like that? She couldn't be serious.

I let it pass. She was talking about something a day and a half away. A day and a half of this horror would feel like a lifetime.

To change the subject I said, "The colors were as beautiful as you said they'd be."

"I'm glad. I wish I could have seen them."

"By the way, your globes have developed little specks at their centers."

"Oh, good."

"Good?"

"It's part of the process."

"What-?"

"I'm tired now, mother. I need to sleep. You should sleep too."

"Oh, yes, well, right..."

Dismissed again.

"Night, Mother."

"Good night, Ellie."

I backed out in a daze, nearly undone by the surreality of the situation...saying a casual-sounding good night to my daughter who'd been turned into some sort of hideous arachnid and was hanging onto the wall of a cave at the end of a passage to some sort of alternate dimension. Was I losing my mind, or was it already gone?

Back in the room I noticed that the specks within the globes seemed larger. A closer look showed they had indeed grown, and had sprouted many wriggly little legs.

Hari

They'd rented two rooms–*two*–at the Renaissance on State Street in downtown Albany, had a big dinner of steaks and a delicious Ripasso, and then she and Donny went their separate ways.

Hari had just finished rearranging the umpteen pillows on her king-size bed and settled back to browse the movie selections when someone knocked on her door.

"Now what?" she muttered as she padded across the room and peeked through the peephole.

Donny.

She pulled open the door and there he stood with a bucket of ice and a very large bottle of Patrón Silver.

"Room service," he said with a grin.

If he was thinking he could ply her with tequila and join her between the sheets, he had another think coming. He didn't know about her hollow leg. But the tequila looked good.

The room was listed as "deluxe"–hey, Art was paying–and had a little sitting area. Very soon they were relaxing with glasses of Patrón on the rocks.

"So let me ask you something," Donny said.

Hari made a face. "Are you going to ruin this with chatter?"

"Seriously, I like to get to know the people I'm working with."

Here we go: Let's see if we can soften her up.

"Why?"

"I just do. So tell me: Are you a cat person or a dog person."

"Do I look like a cat lady?"

"I said 'person.'"

"Neither."

"No pets?"

"Didn't say that. I have a pet crab."

"Can we be serious, maybe just for one minute?"

"I *am* serious. Her name is Pokey and she's an Atlantic blue crab. *Callinectes salpidus*. Means 'beautiful swimmer.'"

His face took on a look of wonder. "You're serious."

"I am. Pokey and I got off to a rocky start. I added her to my fish tank and she gobbled up a couple grand worth of tropicals I had there. I was planning on sautéing and eating her as a soft shell during her next molt but grew attached. I can't say we're good buddies, but we've achieved détente."

His expression remained dubious as he added more Patrón to both their glasses. "Seriously? You have a pet crab?"

"I believe I've answered that."

He said nothing for a few heartbeats, then, "Okay, this is where you ask me about my pets."

"I don't think so."

"Why not?"

"Because I don't care about your pets."

Okay, that sounded harsh. She hadn't said it to hurt him, and she might have found a gentler way to phrase it were it not for the tequila mixing with the wine from dinner–*in vino veritas* and all that–but no matter: It rolled right off him and he launched into a lengthy discourse on how he'd always had a dog as a kid and would have one now if his schedule would allow it, blah-blah-blah. He kept the tequila flowing while he rambled.

His eyelids were at half-mast as he concluded his doggy dissertation with a jarring non-sequitur: "The Septimus people have marked someone for death."

"Whoa!" Hari said. "Where did that come from?"

"I was visiting a dark web chatroom last night and this guy who calls himself 'Belgiovene' said it looked like he was going to be doing 'another freebee.' I've been tracking this guy since February when he talked about an 'easy-peasy freebee' that involved pushing a guy into the Hudson and watching him go down for the third time. That's exactly how Russ died."

"Your brother?" Hari remembered the name from yesterday. "You think he killed your brother?"

"Sure as I can be without actually witnessing it. When someone asked him why for free, he said an organization he belongs to targets a person now and then and taps him to do the dirty work."

"And you think that organization is Septimus?"

He shrugged. "The timing and everything else fits."

He started to pour himself more Patrón but she stopped him.

"I think you've had enough. You're already slurring."

"You're right. I don't want it to affect my performance."

"What performance?"

"You know–you and me...later."

"Oh, you've definitely had too much."

"No, just enough."

"You do realize, don't you, that I'm old enough that, had I been a promiscuous teenybopper, I could be your mother?"

He blinked. "You're saying you're fifteen years older than me–so that makes you, what, like, forty?"

"*I*–older than *I*. And yes, I'm guessing fifteen is about right."

He gave a lopsided grin. "Well, you sure don't look it. I'd put you at thirty, tops."

She repressed a laugh. Yeah, right.

"Flattery will get you everywhere–almost." She grabbed his arm and pulled him to his feet. "Off to bed with you, my friend."

He grinned. "*Just* what I was talking about!"

She opened her door and guided him into the hall. "I mean *your* bed–*alone.*"

"What?" He looked genuinely shocked. "You mean we're both in this nice hotel far from home and we're not going to hook up?"

"I commend you on your grasp of the situation."

"Well, at least walk me back to my room."

"I already have." She pointed across the hall. "There's your door."

Now he put on a hurt face. "Seriously?"

"Don't take it personally, I just don't like beards."

He rubbed his stubbled jaw. "No?"

"They chafe my thighs."

She quickly closed the door to hide an evil grin.

Let him take *that* to bed.

TUESDAY—MAY 16

Hari

"Do you feel as bad as you look?" Hari said as Donny dropped into the passenger seat.

She knew she probably didn't look so hot either. She never slept well in a strange bed, and last night had been especially restless.

"Worse," he mumbled. He looked around. "Hey, I don't remember having an SUV yesterday."

He looked different somehow…and then Hari realized he'd shaved his stubble.

Oh, no. Did he really think they might "hook up," as he'd put it? She'd always hated that term.

She decided not to mention the facial hair. The truth was, part of her restlessness had involved wondering if she should have let him into her bed. She might have fifteen or so years on him, but they were both adults, far from home, as he'd said. Where was the harm?

The harm was in getting involved with a co-worker. Highly unprofessional. And, bottom line, Hari considered herself a professional.

And even if they weren't co-workers, he didn't recognize Deputy Dog or the B-52s.

Hey, Nineteen had started playing in her head again.

"I switched cars first thing this morning," she said. "Deputy Dog–if he's really a deputy at all–might remember our Taurus if he sees it again. Also, the Tahoe here has off-road capability."

Donny didn't seem to be listening. "Can we get some coffee?"

"You read my mind."

Hari already had a couple of cups percolating through her system, but she could always do with more.

They stopped at the same strip mall as yesterday. Hari got four coffees at the espresso shop while Donny hit the Taco Bell for breakfast Crunchwraps, whatever those might be. Then on to the FedEx lot where they set up watch on the Sirocco building from the same spot as yesterday.

The Crunchwraps turned out to be delicious, but she'd barely finished hers before the trucks started rolling, each tractor hauling a new semi.

"Good thing we got here early," Donny said.

Hari started the Tahoe and followed the third truck out of the industrial park.

"We're not gonna wait for the whole convoy?" he said.

Hari shook her head. "I'm operating on the assumption they're going back to Norum Hill. We're going to get there way ahead of them, even before Deputy Dog arrives. He can't keep us off the mountain if we're already there."

"Yeah, but he can kick us off when he finds us."

"Not if he doesn't know we're there."

"I sense that someone has a plan."

"You sense correctly. Let's just hope it works."

She stayed with the convoy until it reached 787, then passed the leaders and raced north to Route 2 where she pushed her speed as much as she dared until they reached Norum Hill. No sign of a sheriff's unit as they wound their way to the top.

"Okay," Donny said as the tires crunched across the gravel of the summit parking area. "We're here. Now what?"

Hari kept the Tahoe moving toward the cell tree at the far northern end of the lot as she said, "We go over the edge."

"No-no-no!" Donny cried, slamming his hands against the dashboard. "Are you crazy?"

"Possibly."

Yesterday, as she'd driven the perimeter of the lot in search of the missing trailers, she'd noticed how the northern end had a gentle grade off the edge, easing down to a line of brush before the trees took over. Whoever had flattened the summit a generation or two ago must have pushed the excess earth off the edge.

Hari bumped the Tahoe over one of the low, concrete parking stops by the cell tree and eased down that grade, stopping in the low brush thirty or forty feet below the summit.

"This is why I wanted four-wheel drive," she said.

Donny had turned in his seat and was staring back up at the summit. "But he'll see us here."

"A good chance he won't. The road up is on the other side of the hill, so we're not visible from there. I suspect Deputy Dog drives up to the summit and checks the lot. If he sees anybody, he shoos them off with some lame excuse. If it's empty, he turns around and goes back down the road and stations himself where he stopped us yesterday."

"Let's hope you're right."

"If he drives the lot perimeter, we're busted, but I'm betting he doesn't."

As they sat with the windows open and listened, Donny fired up his tablet.

"Hey, a new signal report."

"From that Burbank at the Allard?"

"Yeah. Gives me an idea."

"An idea...it's good to know you're open to new experiences."

"Ha-ha." He gave her a pointed look. "More so than you, that's for sure."

"Are you carrying a grudge about last night?"

"Last night?" he said, all innocence. "What happened last night?"

"Nothing. Absolutely nothing." Time to change the subject. "What's your idea?"

"The report gives the coordinates of each frequency it mentions. I'm just wondering if there's one nearby. First let me get our own coordinates..."

He tapped around while Hari kept her ears alert for the sound of tires on the gravel above and behind them.

"I'll be damned," he muttered. "There's one right here on Norum Hill."

"One of those signals?"

Hari found that unsettling. An electromagnetic impulse beaming out of nowhere and striking the Earth right where she was sitting.

"Exactly where?" she said.

"Somewhere down the hill a ways."

"You think it's connected with where they're hiding the trailers?"

A shrug. "How can I say? Might just be an oddball coincidence."

"Or it might not. I–" She held up a hand as she heard a crunching sound.

Definitely tires on the parking area gravel–crunching briefly, then fading away.

"I think that was him," she said, not exactly sure why she was whispering. She slapped Donny on his shoulder. "Let's go."

"Go where? The trucks can't be here yet."

"I want to see if we can find a vantage point that shows us where they leave the trailers."

Keeping below the level of the summit, they made their way through the trees on the south face to where they had a view of a short segment of the mountain road. They crouched and waited. Soon the roar of tractor engines fighting the upgrade echoed through the air, but no trucks rolled into sight. And then the engine noise faded to silence.

"What the hell?" Donny said. "Where'd they go?"

Hari was wondering the same thing. "Maybe they turned their engines off?"

"Truckers don't turn off their engines until they're done for the day–less stress on the diesel to leave it running."

"And you know this how?"

"I just know it."

She shook her head sadly. "But you don't know Deputy Dog."

"And you don't know lolz and slime. But whatever, I'm telling you these guys don't turn off their engines." He rose. "I'm going down there."

Hari pulled him back. "You're doing no such thing. The drivers came back down the hill yesterday, they'll go back down today. And when they do, we'll be close behind. Today we get some answers."

Half an hour later the rumble of the engines returned–not abruptly, but gradually, swelling to a roar.

"Now!" Hari said. "Back to the car."

They hurried to the Tahoe. Its four-wheel drive pulled them up the grade and back onto the gravel.

"Can that tablet of yours show us how close we are to the local signal?"

"Sure. I can compare our GPS coords to the signal's."

"Do it, then. I'm betting the trucks and signal are connected."

She took it slow from there, virtually coasting down the incline. The trucks had departed but the tire marks on the pavement left no doubt where they'd turned on and off the mountain road.

"Same place as yesterday!" Donny said, hammering the dash-board with a fist. "Same dead end!"

"We're missing something," Hari said, cringing at the obviousness of the statement. "How close are we to the signal?"

Donny checked his tablet. "Holy crap. We're almost on top of it."

Pretty much what she'd expected. "I'm going in."

No walking this time. She turned the Tahoe into the gap in the trees and crept ahead along the well-worn ruts. But instead of running into the wall of solid rock they'd faced yesterday, they found a wide opening through the granite.

"Okay," Donny said. "This is spooky. How does this happen? And by the way, this spot matches exactly with the signal coords."

Of course it did. Hari made no comment as she kept the Tahoe rolling forward.

Donny's voice jumped an octave. "We're going *in*?"

"If the trucks can do it, so can we. We go in, take a quick look, then haul our butts back out."

She needed to know what was in there. She couldn't leave until she did.

Driving through the divide was like threading a narrow canyon—a dark canyon, so dark she had to turn on the Tahoe's headlights.

"How long is this thing?" Donny said.

Before Hari could respond, the stone walls fell away and they emerged from the passage into dim light. She slammed on the brakes when she saw what lay ahead.

"Oh, my god!" Donny cried, his voice reaching for a scream. "Get us outa here, Hari! Get us the fuck outa here!"

Barbara

I opened my eyes and stared at the glowing red numbers on the bed-side clock: *11:47*. I jerked my head up for a better look.

What?

Yes. A quarter till noon. I'd overslept. Not that I had anything in particular to be up and about for. Well, Ellie, of course, but she wanted to be alone, so no use in getting up early for her.

But I never slept this late. *Never*. Plus I'd fallen asleep in my clothes. I must have been more exhausted than I'd thought.

I threw off the comforter and padded to the kitchen where I put the kettle on for tea. While the water heated, I checked Ellie's room to see if anything had changed. Out of habit, I knocked before enter-ing, just in case she'd come back through the passage.

"Ellie?"

As expected, no answer, so I pushed through and stepped inside. I glanced at the arch of her construction-the same dark opening as yesterday-then at the window.

The globes were still there but now they were crammed full of dark shapes and countless frantically wriggling legs. I cried out and recoiled, backing against the door and slamming it shut.

Vibrations from the slam caused the globes to jiggle, and then...

I watched in horror as they loosened from the sill and tumbled in a cascade to the floor on the far side of the bed where I couldn't see them.

In the ensuing silence I reached behind me for the doorknob but before turning it I realized Ellie had entrusted these globes to me. I needed to check on them. Just a peek. Carefully, I stepped up onto her bed and edged toward the far side.

Oh, God, they were out. The globes had smashed and the floor was a writhing, undulating carpet of black wriggling forms the size of marbles, marbles with legs, so many legs, and they were...they were eating the broken fragments of the globes.

Slowly, carefully, I backed off the bed and stepped toward the door, but before I reached it they were everywhere, swarming over the bed and under it and around it and flowing toward me in a wriggling black wave. I was barefoot but even with shoes I'd have been defenseless. They surrounded me, blocking my route to the door, and as they closed in I screamed.

And then a voice echoed down the passage.

"That is my mother and she is not to be touched!"

The black swarm froze.

And then the voice said, "Come to me now. Come to me, my kiddlies."

The black wriggling wave turned en masse and raced through the arch into the passage where Ellie waited.

I stood frozen, awestruck, horrorstruck.

Kiddlies...she'd called them her kiddlies.

And then I screamed again as the boiling kettle let out a high-pitched whistle.

Hari

"Wh-where are we?" Hari said as she stared through the windshield at the alien vista.

"I don't know!" Donny said, the words still in his upper register as they came tumbling out, "but this isn't Earth, so turn around and get us the fuck outa here!"

That was Hari's first instinct as well–get out. And she would do exactly that. But not just yet.

"Hold on, okay? Just hold on and get a grip."

They'd passed from bright, late-morning daylight to some sort of purple twilight, from a forested hillside to a huge, broad, bare, mountain-rimmed plateau. They'd answered the question of the semis' whereabouts–at least a hundred were arrayed before them–but Hari had no inkling as to *her* whereabouts.

"What is *that*?" she said, pointing to the giant, red-glowing orb that hung over the darkening horizon.

"I'm gonna guess that's what passes for the sun here," Donny said, his voice shaking. "Wherever 'here' might be. Hari, please–"

"That's not a sun."

"The sun's a star and that's a star–either a red dwarf that we're very close to, or a red giant that's far away. I'm going with close-to-the-dwarf because we haven't frozen yet."

Red giant...red dwarf...they meant next to nothing to Hari... terms she'd seen in the Science section of the Tuesday *Times*. Astronomy-geek talk. The star out there took up a full thirty degrees of the sky and glowed a bright crimson–not bright enough, though, to keep Hari's eyes off it.

She said, "Okay...say you're right. How did we get to another planet?"

"Through that fucking passage, which we should be going back through right now!"

"But all the trailers are here. Septimus is hiding them on another planet?"

"Okay, maybe not on another planet per se, but definitely not on our Earth. Maybe this is another version of Earth. One I don't wish to stay on."

"'Another version'?"

"Yeah. The multiverse. An infinite number of alternate realities. Can we leave now?"

Hari twisted in her seat to look back at the dark opening in the sheer rocky wall behind them. Then back to the trailers.

"Just as soon as we see what's inside those trailers."

With that she turned off the engine, pulled the keys from the ignition, and jumped out.

Donny wailed, "Hariiiiii!"

"If you check a tanker while I'm checking a freight load, we'll be done in half the time and on our way."

Behind her a door slammed and Donny said, "I hate you!"

Hari felt for him. Their situation was beyond frightening, surging into terrifying, mind-boggling, and way beyond, but she'd made this trip to find answers and she wasn't leaving here without them.

"Seriously," Donny said as he caught up with her. "If we get out of this alive, I'm going to kill you."

She pointed to the nearest tanker. "See what's in there."

She trotted to the rear of the closest semi and felt winded by the time she reached it. Was the air thinner here?

She examined the rear swing doors where she found the lock shafts engaged but not padlocked.

And why would they be? she thought. No one's going to steal anything here.

She grabbed the lever handle and swung it out, rotating the long shaft. It popped free and she tugged on the door, swinging it open to reveal neat rows of boxes stacked floor to ceiling. The light wasn't great and so it took her a moment to decipher the printing on the sides. She backed away when she realized what it was.

She called out to Donny. "Freeze-dried food!"

Donny had opened a spigot on the bottom of a tanker and clear liquid was gushing out. He stuck a hand into the flow and raised it to his lips.

"Water!"

She shivered. The air was colder here. But no matter, she had all she needed to know.

"Let's get out of here!"

But as they hurried back to the Tahoe she noticed something that damn near stopped her heart. Donny obviously noticed it too as they both simultaneously skidded to a halt.

"Hey!" he said. "Where's the opening?"

The passage they'd come through was gone. The dark cleft in the mountainside had closed over and they now faced a wall of solid, unbroken rock.

Ernst

Ernst found Slootjes in the lodge basement, hunched over his desk, fairly engulfed in books and scrolls. The loremaster squinted up at him through a pair of bifocals.

"I can tell by your expression you've read it," he said.

Ernst nodded. "It's...harrowing."

Indeed. Charles Atkinson–if such a person truly existed–told his tale in a plain-spoken, matter-of-fact tone that compelled belief. Ernst looked for a place to drop the envelope with the damning memoir but every horizontal surface was occupied.

"Just drop it on the floor," Slootjes said.

Ernst did that, then leaned over the desk.

"Tell me you've debunked this travesty."

Ernst wanted nothing more than to hear a resounding *Yes*. Instead, Slootjes gave his head a slow, sad shake.

"Just the opposite, I'm afraid." He indicated a loose-leaf binder. "I checked with your grandfather's reports to the Council and he often mentions a 'Charles' as being close to Tesla."

"Anyone working with Tesla at the time might have known of this Charles and impersonated him."

"True. But Atkinson's dates regarding the Order's takeover of the financing of the tower experiments jibe with the Council's financial records."

"But–"

"The Council kept its involvement *secret*, Ernst, and we know Tesla never went public with it. The records show they spent a considerable amount of money to keep Tesla going–to the tune of one hundred and twenty-five thousand dollars. Which sounds like a pittance these days, but when you adjust for inflation it comes to three and a half million. That's what the Council poured into the Wardenclyffe project."

"So that part's true," Ernst said. "How did they justify the expense?"

"According to the minutes of the Council meetings in 1903 and thereabouts, the members had read newspaper reports of strange occurrences that sounded like intrusions of Otherness in the Shoreham area along Long Island's North Shore. They investigated and found good reason to believe that Tesla's tower was not only transmitting wireless energy, but thinning the Veil as well. That was why they put up the money."

"And got nothing in return."

"You can't blame them for thinking it a good investment. Look at this."

He led Ernst to the far side of the room where a large map running from Manhattan to the tip of Long Island lay spread out on a ten-foot table. He tapped a spot on the North Shore.

"This was the location of Tesla's Wardenclyffe tower. You will notice that, whether by accident or design, it's also the location of a nexus point. As you know, the Veil is particularly thin at a nexus point. Everything pointed to funding the Serb's experiments as being a worthwhile investment."

Ernst noticed a number of little red bull's eyes scattered on the map.

"What are those?"

"Those are the locations of the area's signals. I don't know if you've been reading the daily updates but all the wavelengths are on the verge of synchronization."

Ernst was well aware convergence was imminent. "I'm surprised there's not a signal at the Wardenclyffe location."

Slootjes shook his head. "The signals didn't begin until 1941, long after Tesla had abandoned Wardenclyffe and the tower was torn down." He tapped the Lower East Side of Manhattan. "There is, however, a signal in Alphabet City, right where that Winslow hack lives. Has he been dealt with yet?"

Ernst didn't care about Winslow now. He placed his hand over the Wardenclyffe location on the map. He could almost feel a part of his family history pulsing there.

"So they sent my grandfather out to oversee the project."

"Yes. As the top actuator in the Order, he was transferred from Germany specifically for that purpose. He set everything in order, and when he showed the council two dead chew wasps from the other side, it only bolstered their confidence that they were on the right track. I don't know if you noticed or not, but Atkinson describes the chew wasps perfectly, even describes the broom-handle Mauser C-96 Rudolph Drexler used to shoot them."

"We have photos of my grandfather with the chew wasps and the Mauser right here in these archives. A spy could have seen them."

"Agreed," Slootjes said. "But what these archives don't have is the slightest hint that Rudolph Drexler was involved with Gavrilo Princip."

Ernst had seen that mentioned in the memoir. He knew from his father that, before leaving for America, grandfather Rudolph had been stoking the fires within a young Bosnian Serb named Gavrilo Princip. The Order eventually relocated the young man to Sarajevo where he assassinated Archduke Ferdinand and precipitated the First World War.

Ernst's own father had saved Hitler's life during the Munich putsch in 1923. Good thing, too: Had the "strutting little Austrian *Gefreiter*," as his father called him, died then, World War II might never have happened.

The brothers of the Ancient Septimus Fraternal Order had spent millennia manipulating people and events to maintain a certain level of dread, despair, and chaos in human affairs, all in an ongoing effort to make the world a more comfortable place for the One and pave the way for the Change. They learned later that they had started the two world wars for nothing. The One had been imprisoned all that time–locked away by an agent of the Enemy for five hundred years. The instant his prison was compromised in the spring of 1941, the signals began.

And now the signals were indicating that the One's time of ascendance was at hand.

Now.

Slootjes was rattling on… "I had to call the Munich Lodge to check on Rudolph Drexler's involvement with Princip, and they confirmed it. Charles Atkinson could have learned of it only from the horse's mouth, so to speak."

Ernst felt his stomach coiling into a knot. "So…the memoir is accurate."

"Everything I checked has been verified."

"Which means I have to accept his description of my grandfather's horrible death as accurate?"

"I'm afraid so. And not only that: When Atkinson says he and your grandfather witnessed horrors beyond the Veil, and that your grandfather concluded that the Order had been duped, I see no choice but to assume he's telling the truth."

"He could have misinterpreted whatever he really said."

Slootjes nodded slowly. "Possible, possible." He looked up at Ernst with a tortured expression. "But if Rudolph Drexler was right, then my whole life has been a lie." He looked away. "I have some deep thinking to do."

"About what?"

"About my responsibilities as loremaster and what my next step should be."

"Meaning?"

"I need time to think. Alone. Please be so kind as to shut the door on your way out."

With nothing more to say, Ernst left the loremaster to himself.

Hari

Donny returned from the base of the mountain wall shaking his head.

"Not a sign of an opening, or that there'd ever *been* an opening. We are so fucked!"

"Be calm," Hari said.

Donny threw his arms up. "How can I be calm when we're trapped on another fucking planet?"

That had been Hari's first thought too, but then she realized...

"Temporarily, yes, but we know that gateway is going to open again."

"Do we?"

Hari struggled for patience and to keep her voice level. She was upset too, but somebody had to set the tone, and it looked like the job had fallen to her.

"Yes, Donny, we do. The truckers seem to be making daily trips, which tells me the gateway opens and closes on a schedule and someone out there knows it."

"But *we* don't."

"We're two smart people. We should be able to figure the interval–I'm betting it's got something to do with the signal that's right outside the gateway–and even if we don't figure it out, all we have to do is wait."

"And keep from freezing to death." He rubbed his arms. "Did it just get colder?"

"Feels that way. Darker too."

She turned to face the enormous red sun and saw its lower quarter had dipped below the horizon.

"Damn, that thing moves fast."

"How long are the nights here?" Donny said. "We have no idea. At least we have the Tahoe's heater to keep us warm."

"But do we have enough gas? We started out with a full tank but do we have enough left to last the night?"

Donny stepped toward the rear of the Tahoe. "I'm going to check for an emergency kit. They might have flares."

"Who are we going to signal?"

"Just give me a minute." He flipped up the rear hatch and rummaged around. "Here we go. Jumper cable–yeah, right, like that'll be useful. Tow rope–no use. Ice scraper–let's hope it's no use. Collapsible shovel–no use unless we need to bury one of us."

"Please!" Hari said.

"Ah! Two flares. Good for heat and light and starting a fire."

A cold wind had sprung up. The sun was two-thirds gone. Hari took a look around the steadily darkening plateau and saw only flat rock. Not a tree, not a bush, not a blade of grass.

"Hate to be a Debbie Downer, but there's nothing here to burn."

"Hey, even I know Debbie Downer. And we can always burn the Tahoe. Look here."

He held up what looked like a large square of folded aluminum foil.

"We're going to wrap sandwiches?" she said.

"Survival reflecting blanket. This'll help us save gas." As he slammed the rear hatch, he looked up. "Shit."

"What?"

He pointed at the sky. "Take a look and tell me what you see up there."

The sun had disappeared and all Hari saw was unrelieved blackness.

"Nothing."

"Exactly."

"Well, it *is* night."

"No stars, Hari. Not one freaking star up there. Where the fuck are we? I mean, where in the universe is this planet that there are no visible stars? Or is it even *in* our universe?"

Hari had no answer and she wasn't about to make up one.

Just then, green lights started wavering across the sky.

Hari pointed. "Those look like–"

"The Northern lights. Or for all we know they could be the Southern Lights here. It's a sign this planet has a magnetic field that's protecting us from at least some radiation."

Hari nodded appreciatively. "You know all sorts of good nerdy stuff, don't you."

"Mostly useless nerdy stuff."

"Either that or you're an excellent bullshitter."

"Actually, I'm a pretty bad bullshitter."

Hari had come to that conclusion the day they'd met.

They stared as the aurora grew brighter and greener, undulating like curtains in a breeze, until Hari shivered in the wind. As beautiful as they were, the lights weren't keeping her warm. She blew on her hands.

"Let's get inside before we freeze our butts off.

Once settled in their seats, Hari started the engine and turned the heat up to max. The fuel gauge read three-quarters of a tank and the dashboard gave them a range of 322 miles. Who cared how many miles were left in the tank; it had now become a question of how many hours.

Donny pulled out his tablet.

"And before you say it," he said, "no, I don't expect to find cell service or a wi-fi hotspot here. But I can work with what's already downloaded and I have all the latest signal reports in memory."

Hari peered through the windshield. With the sun gone and no moon or stars, the darkness would have been impenetrable if not for the emerald-hued aurora wavering across the sky. She watched the lights, fascinated. She considered forty too young to have a bucket list, but if she ever made one, the Northern Lights would have been near the top. She'd been to Iceland where they have aurorae, but she'd traveled in the summer when the sky never got dark. The sun would set, but never too far below the horizon. The darkest hours came around 2 a.m., and the skies were skim-milk pre-dawn gray then. No aurora visible on that trip. She'd planned to return in winter sometime. Now she wouldn't have to.

She hoped she'd at least have the option.

The reality of their situation crashed in on her. They'd entered a rocky opening in the side of a hill in western Massachusetts and ended up on an alien world. Shock and awe and the rush to make sense of what they were experiencing had held deep terror at bay. But now, sitting in a familiar vehicle and looking out at a totally unfamiliar vista that had them imprisoned for who knew how long…terror came knocking. They were the proverbial strangers in a strange land. They didn't know the rules here.

She turned on the headlights. The beams lit up the semi-trailers arrayed before them. Nothing moved out there. Was this planet inhabited? And if so, by what?

The possibilities only increased her terror.

"How does this happen, Donny? We entered a passage into the side of a cliff on Norum Hill and came out here. That's not possible. And yet...here we are."

"It's not possible by our rules, but maybe those rules have been superseded by others."

"That's not an explanation. And why should new rules start to apply?"

"Remember I told you I tapped into the Septimus Foundation's servers and culled through their emails? They're obviously expecting something apocalyptic to happen when the frequencies align. They have this mantra they repeat to each other over and over and–"

"It wouldn't be a mantra unless they kept repeating it." She waggled a finger at him. "I was raised in a Hindu household. I know these things."

"Pardon my pleonasm. Their mantra goes something like: *It will begin in the heavens and end in the Earth, but before that, the rules will be broken.*"

"What's that–a prophecy? We're dealing with a *prophecy*? When did I fall into a Tolkien movie?"

"This is real, Hari. And when you think about it, the rule that says you can't drive an SUV between planets has been broken."

"But-but-but...it's more than a rule. It breaks all the laws of physics..."

"A law is another name for a rule. By the way, it's getting awfully hot in here."

Was it? She was too chilled to notice. She turned off the engine.

"You've become awfully calm about this."

He shrugged. "I was anything but calm at first. I'm not prone to panic attacks but I was on the verge of one out there, but you brought me down. Thanks for that."

"Any time, but...I did?"

"You were taking a rational approach and so I did too: Put the emotions on hold. Plenty of time to panic later. Do some critical thinking first."

She touched his tablet. "Come up with anything?"

"Maybe." He turned the screen toward her. "From what I can tell, someone assigned numbers to the signals. The one on Norum Hill is designated *two-thirty-seven*. I've gone back through the lists and it seems that since the frequencies started changing, someone from a place called Williamstown–I assume it's in the neighborhood–has been reporting any variation in the *two-thirty-seven* frequency every time the signal occurs, which seems to run every eighteen to nineteen hours."

Hari said, "Soooo...if we go by that, dare we assume a periodicity somewhere in the neighborhood of, say, eighteen hours?"

"We can dare. The trucks made a delivery here yesterday afternoon and again this morning. I don't know the exact times off the top of my head, but the interval seems like roughly eighteen hours and–hey, wait. Uh-oh."

"Don't do that."

They were already trapped on an alien landscape. She didn't need to hear *Uh-oh*.

"My tablet downloaded the latest signal report right before we entered the passage. It says all of the reported signals, including *two-thirty-seven*s, have synchronized their frequencies with the Prime Frequency."

"Why does that rate an 'uh-oh'?"

"What if synching with this Prime Frequency means *two-thirty-seven* won't open the passage anymore?"

Hari's heart clenched. "Now who's Debbie Downer?"

"Sorry." He pointed to the dashboard clock. "It's noonish back in our world. We've been here, what, half an hour? That means–if signal *two-thirty-seven* still opens the passage–"

Hari whacked him on the arm. "Do not mention that again. I'm serious."

"Okay, okay. If we've got the interval right, that means the mountain wall will open at five or six a.m. or thereabouts."

The wind rocked the SUV.

"Let's just hope we don't freeze to death before that."

He stared at her. "Seriously?"

"Very seriously. Because I can't see how we have eighteen hours of running time in the gas tank."

He held up the foil packet. "But we do have this super-duper reflecting survival blanket. We can turn on the engine and the heater intermittently and maintain our body heat under this."

Hari watched askance as he began unfolding the foil blanket. "You're talking about snuggling under that?"

He laughed. "Well, we don't have to 'snuggle,' exactly, but we should stay close. Shared body heat is a tried-and-true method of surviving the cold. They say Eskimos sleep with their huskies on cold nights. On a regular cold night they use one dog; when it's colder they bring in a second dog; and a three-dog night is the coldest of them all."

She couldn't resist. "So I'm a dog?"

"No-no-no! I didn't-"

She waved off his explanation. "Kidding. I guess it's a good thing then this Tahoe has a bench seat up here."

"You haven't asked, but yes, I have heard of Three Dog Night."

"Name one song."

"'Joy to the World,' so there's hope for me yet." He handed her a corner of the foil. "Get under this-up to your chin and tuck your feet up under you while I skootch over."

As their shoulders bumped, she said, "Don't get any ideas."

"Oh, believe me: Being stranded on another planet is not my idea of a first date."

"Yeah, you really know how to show a girl a good time."

Frankie

P. Frank Winslow pulled page sixty-two out of the typewriter and added it to the pile, then leaned back and considered the stack of pages he'd typed. Averaging two hundred-fifty words per page, that came to 15,000 words. In less than *one day!* In all his years of writing he'd never done that. Never even come close.

Admittedly, it hadn't been a typical day. He hadn't slept a wink, hadn't eaten a morsel since his arrival in whatever and wherever this was. With no fatigue and no hunger, he'd surrendered to the Disease and kept on typing.

He'd taken breaks to stretch his legs and use the bathroom and give his fingers a rest. The tips were sore from the extra pressure required by the mechanical keys.

When dark had fallen he'd flipped the wall switch and lights came on. Frankie used one break to go up to the roof and scan the city for another lighted window, but couldn't spot a single one.

Earlier in the day, shortly after sunrise, he'd wandered the streets around his building looking for another soul but found no one. Completely deserted. No shops, either. Block after block of blank-eyed apartment buildings, all looking like they'd been furnished by Ikea, all fitted out with heat and electricity and hot-and-cold running water, but no people.

The loneliness and isolation on the street pierced him. Frankie had never been a social person, but also had never realized the subconscious comfort he'd taken in knowing other people were around if he ever felt the need for a little human contact. The loss of that option disturbed him more deeply now than he ever could have imagined.

He hurried back to his building. He didn't need to sleep, didn't need to eat, but he needed to keep writing. He'd already reached novelette length, and at the very least this as-yet-untitled piece was going to be a novella. Maybe even a novel. He didn't know at this point.

What Frankie did know was that he was spinning out the best

thing he'd ever written. Deeper, richer than he'd ever imagined he could produce. Being cut off from humanity had sparked an inferno of thoughts about the human condition, all weaving into a gut-wrenching story. This was going to blow readers' minds. He'd have to come up with yet another pseudonym if he wanted it taken seriously, because no one would ever believe P. Frank Winslow or Phillip F. Winter or Phyllis Winstead capable of this.

No hunger, no fatigue, and once-in-a-lifetime inspiration. A writer's dream.

He'd finish it here in this strange, lonely place...and then he'd have to find a way back. Because what was the point of writing the Great American Novel if no one was ever going to read it?

Ernst

Ernst found Slootjes just where he'd expected: at his desk downstairs in the archives. The clutter was even worse than earlier, but the loremaster wasn't poring over the materials. Instead he sat slumped back in his chair, staring off into space. For a heartbeat or two, Ernst thought he might be dead–a heart attack from the stress of the Atkinson memoir–but then his chest moved as he took a breath.

"Saar?"

Slootjes started, then his eyes focused. "Oh...Ernst. Sorry."

"You looked like you were lost in space."

"Lost in thought is more like it." He sounded so tired.

"About what?"

Slootjes pierced Ernst with his sad gaze. "All the lies that are my life."

Ernst blinked. "I'm sorry...what?"

"It's the title of a story I read long ago. I don't recall who wrote it or a single thing about it, just the title. Because I've been living that title."

"I'm not following."

"That memoir, Ernst. It's all true. Your grandfather witnessed the other side of the Veil and realized that he'd been lied to since he joined the Order, and that he'd been lying to the son he was grooming to join the Order. And you, Ernst, your father, Ernst Drexler the first, you've been lied to all your life as well."

"Be careful, Saar."

"Oh, I don't mean your father intentionally lied to you. I'm sure he was convinced the lies he told you were true, and thought he was passing on arcane truths to his son. But they were lies, lies, lies."

"Come now–"

The loremaster slammed his fist on his desk. "It's true! It's the only truth we have now! We are dupes! We are fools! And thanks to this stranger who met your grandfather, at last we know it. Which leaves me in a very awkward position."

Ernst frowned. "I don't understand."

"Well, as loremaster I must pass this on to our brothers."

Alarm bells rang in Ernst's brain. "Pass what on?"

Slootjes had a strange look in his eyes. "Your grandfather's fate and the doubts he had about the Order's mission. I confess to having had my own doubts deep down over the years, but this confirms them."

"Let's not do anything rash. I'll call a Council meeting to discuss–"

"Discuss? *Discuss?* The Council is peopled with dolts! Nothing but gullible dolts who believe every lie the One feeds them!"

"You shouldn't talk about the One that way. If he hears–"

"And where *is* the One? Has anyone heard from him lately? He's dropped out of sight. Maybe he's in hiding. Maybe even *he's* afraid of what the Change will bring!"

Good question. Where was the One? Two months had passed since Ernst's last contact with him. Maybe the stars had to align or the spheres of the multiverse had to rotate into a certain configuration. Who could say? The convergence of the signals indicated that the Change was about to begin.

Of all living members of the Order, none had provided the One more personal service toward bringing the Change than he, Ernst Drexler. He and the upper echelons of the Order expected to be rewarded in the world that followed the Change. As for the fate of brothers like the loremaster and the rank-and-file members, Ernst was not so sure.

But the One's silence these past months as everything came to a head…Ernst found it not only puzzling, but deeply disturbing.

"Please be calm, Saar–"

"The time for calm is long gone! I'm going to gather my notes and,, first thing tomorrow, I'm going to send out a worldwide email blast to the membership. Everyone should be prepared for betrayal. I may have been fooled like the rest of the Order, but now that I know the truth, I will not betray my trust, I will not betray my brothers."

"Listen to me–"

"You want me to cover it up? That's what you're saying, isn't it? How typical of an actuator. The Order above everything. Septimus *über alles* and to hell with the members!"

He was working himself into a froth of anger.

"I want you to think this through."

"The time for believing in lies is done. The time for truth is at hand." He strode to the door and yanked it open. Pointing to the stairwell outside, he cried, "The archives are my domain and you are no longer welcome here, Actuator Drexler. Out!"

"But–"

"*OUT!*"

At a loss as to how to defuse the situation, Ernst stepped into hall. After the door slammed behind him, he heard the lock turn.

Slootjes had gone mad. Mad with fear? Mad with hate? Ernst couldn't say. But whatever the cause, Ernst could not let him send out that email tomorrow. A loremaster, however, answered only to the Council itself. Ernst would have to alert them.

Hari

Hari hated hotel beds and this had to be the most uncomfortable pillow ever. But when she banged her fist against it to soften it up, she heard a voice nearby say, "Ow!"

She opened her eyes and realized her head was on someone's lap. And through that someone's jeans she could feel an erection pressing against the back of her head.

"Whoa!" she said, jerking upright to face Donny. The foil blanket fluttered around them. It all came back in a rush. "How did that happen?"

"You conked out," Donny said.

"And landed on you?"

"It was sort of a slow-motion fall."

She looked around. Nothing had changed: the green aurorae still flickered in a starless sky. How long had she been out? The reflective blanket, augmented by intermittent blasts from the Tahoe's heater, had been keeping them comfortable. Too comfortable, apparently. Sleep deprivation had caught up to her.

"Why didn't you wake me?"

He waved his hands. "I'm a firm believer in catching as many winks as you can whenever you can. And besides, I kind of liked it."

She gave the bulge under his fly zipper a quick pat. "'Kind of'?"

"Do *not* do that!" he said, pressing his knees together.

"I'm not a cougar, and are you really that horny?"

"Only when you're around."

She had to laugh. "I know it's dark but did you happen to see my eyes roll?"

"No, but I heard them."

Hari couldn't say exactly why–not even approximately why–but his perfect quip seemed to flip a *Why not?* switch in her and she gave in to an insane impulse.

"Oh, hell," she said and leaned over and kissed him on the lips.

He responded and soon their tongues were dueling and their hands were roving and she was rubbing that bulging fly and his fingers had just closed around one of her breasts when something went *thump!* against the passenger side of the car.

The heat growing within Hari flash-froze to ice.

"What was that?" she said. "There's not supposed to be anything moving out there."

"Tell me about it. Maybe it was just the car settling or–"

Hari suppressed a scream when she saw the slim black tendril sliding up the rear window.

"Where'd *that* come from?" she whispered.

"Oh, shit!" Donny said, also keeping his voice low. He pressed the side of his face against the passenger window for a better look. "Oh, *shit!*"

"What-what-what?" She didn't want to know but she had to know. "What is it?"

"It looks like a giant clump of crude oil that's washed up from a tanker spill, except it's moving...oozing out pseudopods like an amoeba."

What?

"This isn't a time for jokes, Donny."

"Who's joking? It's partially under the car and it's *big*, Hari. You can probably see it on your side too."

Hari hesitated, then peeked out her window.

Donny's description had been right on the money: an amorphous flattened blob with a glossy tarry surface reflecting the aurora. It moved like an amoeba, extending pseudopods then flowing into them. Here and there a black, antennalike tendril jutted from its surface and undulated in the air. One of these had struck the rear window.

A dozen feet beyond this one she spotted another dark shape slithering along the ground.

"I see it," she said. "And it's not alone. But where do they come from? The ground is solid, no nooks or crannies or crevices. Where were they hiding?"

Donny said, "Better question: How many are there?"

"One way to find out."

As Hari reached for the steering column, Donny said, "Maybe we ought to–"

She turned on the headlights.

"–think about that–oh, Christ!"

As before, the beams lit up the ranks of semi-trailers. But unlike before, they had glistening ebony creatures crawling over them.

Whatever they were, the plateau appeared to be home to hundreds of these things.

"Are they eating the food?" Donny said.

"The containers inside the trailer I checked showed no damage. Either they can't get in or they don't eat human food–if you can call freeze-dried scrambled eggs and beef Stroganoff human food."

The oil clumps had all been in motion when she'd turned on the lights, but now they froze in place. Even their antenna-tendrils had stopped waving.

"What happened?" Donny said. "Did you scare them?"

"Maybe I should turn the lights off."

"No, wait. They're moving again."

Yes, moving again…the ones climbing the semis reversed direction and oozed toward the ground. And those on the ground…

"Christ, they're heading this way!" He began hammering the steering wheel. "Turn off the lights, turn off the lights!"

Hari was already there. Darkness returned as the headlights died, but green flashes from the aurora-strewn sky reflected off the surfaces of the clumps.

"They're still headed this way," Hari whispered, her mouth going dry. "Why? What do they want?"

"Maybe you triggered some phototropic response."

"But the lights are out."

"Maybe it's sound…or heat." The survival blanket had bunched up during their clinch. He spread it over them again and said, "Get back under here."

Huddling under the blanket made no difference–the things kept coming. Soon they surrounded the Tahoe, reaching up and slapping the fenders and hood and windows with their tendrils.

And then they started crawling onto the vehicle, one after another, slithering up the sides, blocking the auroral light and engulfing the Tahoe in squirming darkness.

"I don't think it's light or heat," Donny said. "It's us they want."

Hari jabbed the door-lock button and said, "They can't get in, can they?"

"I think we're safe."

"What'll happen if we start the engine?"

"Let's not find out."

"We have to get them off us, Donny. How will we know when the passage reopens? And how will we reach it when it does?"

"Maybe they'll get frustrated and go away. Did you happen to notice what time it was?"

Hari hadn't, so she turned the key. The dashboard lit up and the clock read *11:46.*

Donny groaned. "Six hours left."

In the wash from the dashboard lights Hari noticed a number of pale spots on the windshield. She turned on the courtesy lights. Yes...about a dozen pale, dime-sized circles on the glass.

"What's happening here?"

Donny leaned closer. "Almost looks like etching–oh, shit. They're etching the glass!"

"How? Don't you need acid or something to do that?"

"Yeah. Hydrofluoric acid. They look like they're secreting it."

"To etch the glass?" Even as she said it, Hari knew that wasn't right, that the reason had to be more sinister.

"No." Donny's voice quavered. "To burn through it."

WEDNESDAY—MAY 17

Barbara

1

Someone was shaking my shoulder.

"Wake up, Mother. We don't want to be late."

I opened my eyes, blinked a few times, and Ellie came into focus, leaning over me where I must have dozed off on the living room couch. She wore the same clothes as when she'd entered the passage on Monday and–I blinked again–no spider legs in sight.

I rubbed my eyes and looked again. No...no spider legs.

Had I dreamed all that? I couldn't believe my mind capable of concocting such a scenario, even in a nightmare, yet here she was, looking like her old self.

No, not her old-old self. This was the pre-passage Ellie, with the stranger who called me "Mother" looking out through her eyes.

"Ellie...you're all right?"

"As well as can be expected. But come on–rise and shine or we'll be late."

"Late for what?"

"Something momentous: the sunrise."

"That happens every day."

"Not like this, it doesn't. It's scheduled to rise at five twenty-one."

"Good Lord, what time is it now?"

"Three-thirty. We have trains to catch if we're going to reach Coney Island in time."

I rose from the couch and stretched. My back ached from sleeping in an odd position.

"Why Coney Island? That's a long way."

I'd never been there but remembered it lay at the far end of Brooklyn.

"Because standing on a shore and watching the sun rise over the water will allow us to appreciate the full impact."

"Ellie, you're not making any sense."

"Everything will make sense when we're there, Mother. But we can't dilly-dally. The trains are few and far between at this hour. Grab a coat because it's chilly before dawn. And bring your phone because we'll want to watch the time. I'll get Blanky."

"Blanky?"

She turned away and I saw her back. No spider legs, but…

"Oh, God! Oh, dear God!"

My knees gave way and I dropped back onto the couch. Her back was a seething, wriggling black mass of those little…things. They clung to her and to each other, bulking from the base of her neck to her waist.

She glanced back over her shoulder. "What?"

I pointed. "Those…those…" Words failed me.

"Oh, the kiddlies are coming along. They need to get out for a while."

2

For a child–okay, teenager–who'd been to New York only a couple of times, and had never been on the subway, Ellie possessed an uncanny knowledge of its workings. I didn't ask her how. I knew she'd say she'd learned all about it during her coma.

She'd tied Blanky around her neck where it hung over her back like a cape, mercifully concealing her horrid "kiddlies" from me and the few other people scattered on the streets at this hour. As she led me to the Lexington Line station at Seventy-seventh Street, I'd glance at her and catch faint flashes or ghost images of spindly spider legs arching from her back, but they'd be gone before I could focus. Also…Blanky…at times Blanky flickered and transformed into a long, flowing, high-collared red cape like a Disney princess might wear, and then reverted to ratty old Blanky again.

"Where are the…extra legs?" I said.

"Here and not here. Tucked elsewhere. Don't want to attract too much attention, do we?"

Part of me wanted to run–*screamed* to run from her–but another part, the mother part, couldn't leave. This was my child, my baby, and I had to stick by her in this time of trial. She'd changed for the worse–no, I shouldn't say *worse*. She hadn't done anything bad, hadn't hurt anyone. She'd changed to the strange, the uncanny, the bizarre, the frightening. But that didn't mean she wouldn't change back to who she'd been, and I had to be there when she did. Because she'd need me. She didn't seem to need me now, but she'd need me then.

Down in the subway station, after what seemed like a long wait, we caught the six train downtown. We shared our car with a couple of drowsy drunks and a homeless woman stretched out on a bench surrounded by the plastic bags she'd filled with her earthy possessions. I hadn't noticed at the apartment or on the street, but here under the fluorescents of the subway car, Ellie looked pale and drawn. Her cheeks were sunken.

"When did you last eat?" I said.

A wan smile. "Been a while."

But was it more than simply not eating?

"Those...things...they aren't biting you, are they?"

I imagined them sucking her blood like ticks.

"No. They'd never bite me. And they know not to bite you either."

"Well, you need to eat," I said. "At the next stop we'll get out and find an all-night coffee shop and get some nourishment into you."

She gave her head an emphatic shake. "No, Mother. This is a big day. I have to stay on schedule."

"For the sunrise? It will happen whether you're watching or not."

"Sunrise isn't the first stop on the schedule."

"What is?"

"All in good time, Mother."

At Bleeker Street we switched to the D train and continued to the end of the line at Coney Island. Once the D left Manhattan, it stopped being "sub" and traveled on elevated tracks.

After an uneventful trip on two largely uninhabited trains, we reached the end of the line at Coney Island. Ellie led us down to street level where we found ourselves in a rough, seedy neighborhood.

"I don't like it here," I said.

"It's necessary," she said. She was in enigmatic mode now. "What time on your phone?"

I checked. "Four fifty-seven."

"Good. We have time."

"Hey, Red Riding Hood," said boozy male voice. "I dig the cape."

An unshaven man in a short jacket and a fedora set at a rakish angle stepped out of the shadows and approached us.

I tugged on Ellie's sleeve. "Let's go."

But Ellie stood firm, muttering something that sounded like, *Right on schedule.*

"Good evening, sir," she said. "Could you direct us to the boardwalk?"

"Sure can." He stopped two feet before us. "Gimme your fancy red cape and I'll guide you there myself."

It occurred to me that he was seeing the red cape I'd seen in flashes throughout our trip.

"I'm afraid I can't give up Blanky."

"We ain't hagglin', little girl." A knife with a nasty-looking blade appeared in his hand. "Hand it over."

I wanted to run but I couldn't leave Ellie.

"I've had Blanky all my life."

He waved the blade toward me. "This looks like your mother. You've had her all your life too, right? How's about I cut her and we see if you still wanna keep your cape?"

Ellie *tsk*ed. "Well, since you put it that way."

She untied the blanket from around her neck and handed it over. I noticed that her back was clear of the creatures. I glanced at Blanky and saw its entire underside massed with kiddlies.

"Ellie..."

"Mother..." A warning tone.

I zipped my lips.

The man had slipped the knife into his belt and was swinging Blanky over his shoulders, then knotting it around his neck.

"You know, I used to be quite the fashion plate. I had a stable of the finest girls on the street. Then everything went south for me. But I can still look sharp, right? I can–"

His expression suddenly changed–to puzzled, then concerned.

"What the–?"

He started twisting and clawing at his back. He staggered in a circle as he tried to untie Blanky but his fingers fumbled futilely at the knot.

When he turned back to us his eyes were black with crawling things and wriggling legs. He opened his mouth but it was filled with the same. His hands fell to his sides as he dropped to his knees; he swayed back and forth once or twice, then he toppled face-first onto the sidewalk where he lay still. Not a twitch, not a groan. He looked shrunken inside his clothes. His right eye socket–empty now–was visible.

I stared in open-mouthed shock. No doubt he was dead.

"Ellie?" I said when I found my voice, a voice that sounded like someone else's. "What happened?"

"The kiddlies defended us. It just so happened they were hungry as well. They have no taste for skin and bone, but they like everything else."

I closed my eyes and swallowed a surge of bile. She was telling me that he was–quite literally–little more than a bag of bones now.

A couple of commuters hurried by, barely looking at him. Ellie removed Blanky from his corpse–I couldn't help but notice the black, writhing mass clinging to its underside–and retied it around her neck. I shuddered at the thought of those things against my own back.

"Come," she said. "The sunrise awaits."

3

I barely remember the trek up Stillwell Avenue to the boardwalk. Vague images of Nathan's signs and that grinning Steeplechase Face everywhere, a rollercoaster to my left, the bright orange height of the defunct Parachute Jump looming to my right, and finally a locked-up pavilion overlooking the beach and the sparkling water.

"Excellent!" she said, spreading her arms toward the limitless expanse of pristine sky. "A beautiful morning for the show."

I was too numb with shock and, I confess, sick fear to appreciate the weather. A man had died back there. A scum-of-the-earth man, a former pimp from what he'd said, but a human being nonetheless, and he'd been devoured from the inside by Ellie's kiddlies.

And Ellie herself…in the pre-dawn light I could see how her face had filled out and her cheeks now showed a rosy glow.

I realized to my horror that the kiddlies had shared their bounty. Ellie had fed too.

She pointed west, past the Parachute Jump. "See that purplish sky just above the horizon? That's called 'Earth shadow,' which is exactly what it is–a shadow cast by the curve of the eastern horizon before the sun rises above it. And see that pink band above that? That's the sun lighting up the higher levels of the atmosphere. It's called the Belt of Venus."

"Did you learn this in your coma too?"

"No, Mother," she said, her tone arid. "In Mister Benson's astronomy class. What time on your phone?"

I checked. "Five twenty."

She pointed east. "The sun is supposed to appear in one minute."

We waited. A minute passed, then two, then three...and no sun.

"Well, Ellie, either my phone's wrong or your information is wrong."

"Before I woke you, I checked with the U.S. Naval Observatory. Using Eastern Standard Time, it lists today's sunrise at this latitude and longitude at four twenty-one. Since we're in Daylight Saving, I had to add an hour."

Five twenty-five and still no sun.

"This is impossible, Ellie. The sun's never late, and the days are supposed to be getting longer, not shorter."

My phone was reading five twenty-six when a crimson crescent began to peek over the horizon.

"There!" she cried, pointing. "There it is! A wonderful five minutes late! It's begun, Mother! It's truly begun!"

For a few seconds her spider legs appeared—not hazy and ghostly, but sharp and solid enough to click when they touched. They materialized and moved around, then disappeared, all without disturbing Blanky's fabric. But they weren't responsible for the wave of deep unease coursing through me—the sun's tardiness triggered that.

"You knew the sun was going to be late? How?" But I knew the answer.

"I believe I spoke it aloud many times in my coma: It will begin in the Heavens..."

"'And end in the Earth.' Spoke? You'd shout it. But what–?"

She gestured again toward the rising sun. "As predicted, it has begun in the Heavens. This morning the sun rose late. Tonight it will set early. Tomorrow morning it will rise even later. Night is falling, Mother. The Change has begun. His time is at hand."

"Who's time?"

"Why, the One's, of course."

"The One what?"

She looked at the rising sun. "A long story, Mother. Come, you and I will walk the boards, as they say, and I will tell you all about it before I have to return to Manhattan."

"'Have to'?"

She seemed to have all sorts of frames of reference to which I had no clue–more coma learning, I assumed.

"A fraternal order will have need of my services later this morning, but we have plenty of time before I'm due there."

Hari

Hari screamed. She'd sworn to herself that she wouldn't, but when the shiny black tendril extruded through the windshield, the scream burst free unbidden.

They'd tried everything they could think of, even going so far as to start the engine and drive blindly, accelerating, then jerking to a halt in an effort to dislodge the tarry clumps. But no use. They'd somehow glued themselves to the doors and windows and weren't leaving.

She'd watched with growing horror as the acid they secreted ate away at the window glass–not just the dozen or so spots on the windshield, but the side and rear windows as well. On the upside, it proved an agonizingly slow process that took hours upon hours; on the downside, the clumps seemed to have infinite patience.

Adding to the terror was the frustration of watching the clock creep toward 5:30. If, as they predicted and hoped, the passage reopened around that time, they'd have no way of knowing. And even if by some chance they did know, they wouldn't be able to reach it driving blind.

So they sat and watched the deepening pocks on the glass. Only a matter of time before–

And then it happened. The glass thinned to the point where the outside pressure of the clumps penetrated in one...two...three places, allowing tendrils to writhe through. They undulated wildly, angling this way and that as if sniffing the air in search of prey.

Hari pressed herself back as far as the seat cushion would allow. For a rapid heartbeat or two she thought she might have confused the thing, but then, after freezing for an instant, it darted toward her face.

That was when she screamed. She raised her hands in defense and the tendril tip fastened onto her forearm like cold dry lips in an obscene kiss.

"Donny!"

But he was tangled with two of them. And then a fourth and a fifth broke through, searching for nourishment or whatever it was they wanted. A second tendril fastened onto her other arm and Hari screamed again in plain, flat-out horror and despair because she saw their doom snaking all around them and no way to fight back and–

What?

The tendrils stopped their writhing and sucking and froze in position. Then they abruptly retracted through the holes in the glass. As they slid off the windshield, the plateau became visible again. The aurora was gone. The sky had lightened while they were under attack, but they hadn't had a clue. And now the huge red sun was cresting the mountaintops. Despite the alienness of the whole scene, Hari thought she'd never seen anything so beautiful.

"Sunrise..." Donny said, breathless. "You think that's it? Those things only come out at night?"

Hari was checking her forearms. The sucking tips of the tendrils hadn't had a chance to break the skin, but...

"I've got hickies!"

Donny pointed through the Swiss-cheesed windshield. "Hey, look at the oil slick thingies."

The black clumps were flattening themselves, then seeping into the ground like liquid, leaving no trace.

"That's why we had no idea they were here," Hari said. A glance in the rearview mirror made her jerk upright in her seat. "The passage! It's opening!"

She started the engine, rammed into drive, and started a tire-screeching 180 turn.

"Easy, easy," Donny said. "Let's make sure it's completely open before we bowl into it."

Hari could appreciate his concern. The area of the cliff wall that was opening had a misty look that darkened as the red sunlight brightened.

"That's it!" Donny cried. "The star's light triggers the passage."

Hari checked the rearview again. The big red ball was halfway risen. She slowed the Tahoe.

"Let's hope so. I'll keep us at a crawl until it fully clears the horizon. If you're right, we should be good then."

The opening darkened and deepened as more and more of the sun came into view. When it finally looked again like it had when

they'd arrived, Hari eased forward and into the passage. A few minutes later they emerged onto a wooded mountainside with their own
sun, smaller and gloriously yellow, sitting above a forested horizon.

Hari paused for a moment to drink in the delicious familiar-
ity, then turned downhill and drove as fast as she dared to get off
this mountain before the sheriff and the convoy arrived to drop off
another load. She kept a death grip on the steering wheel and didn't
relax until they turned onto Taconic Trail.

"What happened to us back there?" she said, slumping in her
seat. "Were we really on another planet being attacked by living oil
slicks? Or did someone slip some LSD into our morning coffee?"

Donny stuck an index finger through one of the holes in the
windshield.

"We didn't hallucinate these. And–oh, Christ. Look at the hood!"

Hari had been concentrating so much on the twisty mountain
road she hadn't noticed how large patches of the car's paint job had
been corroded away.

"Those things must have been secreting all sorts of acids. How
do we explain this to the rental folks?"

"Vandals," Donny said. "Antifa vandals thought we were
Republicans and attacked us with acid. Works for me."

As they neared the New York-Massachusetts border, they came
upon a convoy of a dozen or so trucks hauling freight and tanker
trailers toward Norum Hill.

"We never got a chance to talk about what they might be up to,"
Donny said.

Hari had barely had time to think, what with all that had happened, but now...

"Tons of freeze-dried food and water to reconstitute it. Pretty
obvious they're planning on feeding people–either a select group for
a long time, or a fair-sized population for a short time. Either way, it's
pretty clear they're expecting an apocalypse."

"But what kind? Environmental? Economic? Viral? Zombies?
What?"

"Check the radio," she said. "See if anything happened while we
were out of touch. Try AM."

"AM?" Donny made a face. "I didn't think anyone still listened
to AM."

"It's your best chance of finding an all-news station."

After a few tries with the scan button it stopped on 810 where they suffered through traffic and weather and sports until Donny reached for the tuner. But Hari grabbed his hand when she heard...

Did the sun rise late today? Most people don't pay that close attention, but the folks at the National Weather Service do. That's their job. And Doctor Claire Berkley, a meteorologist at the National Oceanic and Atmospheric Agency, says that the sun did indeed rise late over Washington, DC this morning–five minutes and eight-point-two-two seconds late, to be precise. Doctor Berkley says it rose late by exactly the same interval at the Greenwich Observatory in England as well, and that it has been rising late all over the world. When pressed for an answer she stated:

"'The only imaginable cause would be a shift in the Earth's axis, which would, conversely, cause an earlier *sunrise in the southern hemisphere. But sunrise was late all over the globe, and Earth's axis is unchanged.'*

"Doctor Berkley said she had no explanation yet. We will be following this incredible story. Meanwhile, in other news..."

"Holy shit!" Donny said. "The sun rose late? *Late?*"

Hari felt a chill, which graduated to tremors as she saw all the dominoes falling. Fearing she'd lose control of the car, she pulled onto the shoulder and skidded to a stop.

"What's the matter? You okay?"

She could only shake her head. Not okay. Not okay at all.

"Hari, are you gonna be sick?"

She found her voice. "What was that mantra you mentioned yesterday, the one in the Septimus Foundation emails?"

Now, Donny looked a little sick himself. "'It will begin in the Heavens...'"

"I think that's just what happened while we were trapped in Wherever: It began in the Heavens. This is what the Septimus folks have been preparing for."

"The sun rising late?"

"I can't see it being a one-time thing. Think about it: the sun rises progressively later every day when it's supposed to be rising earlier. What's the fallout from that?"

"Well, less daylight, for sure."

"Which means crop failures, Donny. Not just local–worldwide. And worldwide crop failures lead to worldwide famine. And how do you prepare for worldwide famine?"

Donny's voice was very small. "Stockpile food."

"Right. For your own people and for others you want to control. When the world goes hungry, the guy serving lunch calls the shots. They've seen this coming and they've been preparing."

"We've got to tell Art."

"Tell Art?" She heard her voice rising but couldn't stop it. "Sure. Tell Art so he can sell off his stocks and collect all that nice cash–for *what?* If this is going to go like they think, it's the end of the fucking world, Donny, or at least the end of life as we know it! We've got signals from outer space or beyond outer space shooting into the Earth and maybe causing all this. We've got a hole through a mountain back there that leads to another planet! What if that passage doesn't close one time and all those tar-clump things decide to migrate to this side? They like the dark and now daylight is shrinking! We are fucked, Donny! Royally fucked!"

She realized she was screaming and shut up.

"Don't lose it, Hari," Donny said with a wide-eyed stare. "Please don't lose it. You're the most together woman I've ever known–make that *person* I've ever known. If you can't hold it together–"

"I'm okay. Just had to vent a little. I'm okay now."

Not true. She wasn't sure she'd ever be okay again–not with what the future promised. But she felt better. The venting had helped some, but only a little. The apocalypse loomed. She had to find her own way to deal with it.

She put the Tahoe in gear and got rolling again.

"You have a plan?" Donny said.

"I'm working on one."

The signals...somehow the signals were key. Or at least a starting point.

"I can't stop thinking about those Septimus sonsabitches," Donny said. "They knew this was coming but they kept it to themselves. Coulda warned the world but instead they're angling to take advantage of the shit storm. Someone needs to take them down."

An uncomfortable thought struck Hari. "You don't happen to own a gun, do you?"

A short harsh laugh. "No. I'm a lover, not a fighter. I couldn't pull a trigger on man nor beast. But someone oughta do something."

"Well, if you'll pardon the cliché, what goes around tends to come around."

He shook his head. "No, it doesn't. It doesn't come around unless someone makes it come around."

Hari decided then she liked him. Liked him a lot.

They spent the rest of the trip in relative silence. Hari didn't know what Donny was thinking, but her own thoughts kept returning to those signals. She remembered the email address that sent the reports because it included an iconic Central Park West apartment building–almost as iconic as the Dakota: *Burbank@theallard.com*. She'd pay a visit to the Allard as soon as she made it back to the city. She hoped "Burbank" referred to a person and not the Los Angeles suburb, because she had a ton of questions about the signals, and was pretty sure this Burbank had the answers.

As they hit the outskirts of Troy, Donny broke the silence.

"Drop me off at one of the airport hotels."

"What? You're staying?"

A nod. "Yeah. Got some unfinished business here."

"Oh? Like what?"

"Let's just leave it at that, okay?"

Was he trying to be mysterious? He wasn't terribly good at it.

"You said someone needs to take Septimus down. You're not planning something stupid, are you?"

He grinned. "Me? Stupid? In a way I wish I were. The thing is, I don't have any sort of plan yet, so I want to stay here and work on one."

"You can work on it back in the city."

"Nope-nope-nope. Their stockpile is here. That's the key to whatever they're planning. That's where I can hurt them."

"You're one guy, Donny, and they're many. They're the kind of people who find some wormhole to another planet and use it to hide their supplies. They operate on a whole different level than we know or can even imagine."

"That's why it's got to be an excellent plan."

Donny was adamant about staying so they stopped at a La Quinta outside the Albany airport. Hari admitted to herself that she was worried about him—worried enough that she accompanied him inside and continued trying during the registration process to talk him into coming back to New York. She even followed him to his room.

"We're better off investigating the signals."

"The signals?" He shook his head. "That's the cosmic end of this. I can't deal with cosmic. What I can deal with is real-world stuff like trucks and trailers. I just have to figure out how."

"Okay, look," she said. "Will you promise me one thing? Promise me you won't get in their faces. Promise me you'll keep arm's length and do whatever you do anonymously. You said yourself these people are dangerous. Look what they did to your brother."

She hated to bring that up, but Donny wasn't some black ops veteran, he was just a hacker, and she had a sense that Septimus ran broader and deeper than either of them could imagine.

His expression darkened. "And that's why they have to pay."

"Have it your way," she said and started to turn away.

"Hey." He spread his arms. "After all we just went through and not even a hug?"

Okay, he had a point.

They clinched but he held on and whispered in her ear. "We could finish what we started on that other world. People have the Mile-High Club. We could inaugurate the Interplanetary Club."

Hari broke the clinch with a laugh. "You never give up!"

He winked. "As Septimus is about to find out."

He keyed his door open and waved as he entered. Hari walked down the hall and out to the parking lot where she stopped and looked up at a sun that had risen late this morning and, if her intuition was right, would set early tonight.

Why was she leaving Donny alone in that room? The world was in the process of ending and here was a good guy—a little young, maybe, but well into adulthood—who truly wanted her. This moment might never come again.

She turned and headed for his room. By the time she knocked on his door, she had her blouse fully unbuttoned. She delighted in his shocked expression when he opened it and saw her

"I've got an hour," she said, pushing him back into the room. "Don't waste it."

Ernst

The sun had risen late.

The Change was upon the world.

At last.

Ernst had been anticipating this any day for the two months since he had last seen the One. Apparently the stars or planets had aligned or the gears of the multiverse had reset. Or not. All that mattered was that it had begun.

The One's time, the Order's time, and most important, *Ernst's* time was at hand. Though he wished the One had given them warning. Even the Council had been left in the dark.

It may have begun in the Heavens as predicted, but instead of basking in the glow of this momentous occasion, Ernst Drexler was forced to deal with the Order's more mundane issues.

Yesterday he'd informed the Council of Slootjes's determination to tell the membership that the Order had been played for fools for millennia, that they'd been misled by the dupes on the Council of Seven who repeated all the lies they'd been fed.

And now this morning, Council member Patel had stopped by the Lodge with a pronouncement: "Loremaster Saar Slootjes has been designated a Threatening Presence."

A loremaster receiving the Threatening Presence designation was unheard of–unprecedented in Ernst's experience. It amounted to a death sentence: a Threatening Presence had to be eliminated at all costs, by whatever means necessary.

Naturally it came down to Ernst Drexler, as the Lodge's actuator, to deal with any member labeled a Threatening Presence. But on today of all days…it didn't seem right.

"The Change has begun," Ernst told Patel. "Surely that makes this all moot."

"Oh, quite the contrary," Patel said. "He will raise doubts about the Order's place in the post-Change world. He will tell them we won't be ascendant in the new order. We can't allow him to create a crisis of faith within the membership. We haven't been stockpiling food for no reason, you know."

Wait...what?

"Stockpiling food? Where?"

"Beyond the Leng passage. There's no place safer."

"Why wasn't I told of this?"

Patel gave his arm a condescending pat. "You're an actuator, Ernst. Not your concern. These matters are best left to the Council."

Officially Patel was right, but Ernst's father had always said an actuator's job was to make things happen for the Order, and this had happened without him.

"I'm hardly rank and file."

"Of course not. But trust me, you wouldn't want to be saddled with the logistics of the problem. I'm constantly arguing and cajoling on the phone. Sometimes I want to hurl it across my office or bounce it off a wall. The truckers up in Albany are chronically behind in moving the shipments to safety, and that's all Brother Riker's fault. His lame excuse is that they can't risk running more than ten trucks to the passage at once for fear of attracting too much attention. And just recently he thinks someone has been following the convoy."

"Still, I wish I'd known."

"And now you do." Another condescending pat. "But don't allow this to distract you. If the supplies aren't secured in time, the rank-and-file members will suffer, not us. Just take care of the Slootjes threat. Inform the Council as soon as it's done."

Ernst didn't feel up to eliminating Slootjes. The loremaster wouldn't be the first member of the Order he'd terminated. But in those cases he'd felt justified because he'd been eliminating a threat, either to himself or the Order. And, coincidentally, in all previous incidences he'd actively disliked, even loathed the target. He rather liked Saar, despite his tendency toward drama queen.

Ernst would take another shot at dissuading him. If that didn't work, he'd bring in Belgiovene.

Frankie

P. Frank Winslow stood in the cab of his building's elevator, trying one key after another in the slot next to the bottom button on the control panel. He'd taken the keyring from the lobby office with no guarantee that it held the one he was looking for.

He was desperate for a way back to his reality. He'd considered going floor to floor and room to room in search of another gap in a floor or ceiling, but put it off. He could always do that. What he couldn't get out of his head was the last button in this elevator. Why was it locked?

Finally one slipped in and turned.

"Yes!" he cried as the cab started down. But down to where?

Well, he'd find out soon enough. For all he knew, it opened into hell itself.

He adjusted the weight of the 172-page manuscript tucked under his arm. Okay, so it wasn't the Great American Novel, but it sure as all hell was the Great American Novella.

He couldn't be sure—not without a word processor to do the counting—but he guesstimated the novella's length at forty-two or forty-three thousand words. He never dreamed he was capable of that kind of output. It seemed almost inhuman. But the words kept flowing faster and faster and his typing kept accelerating to keep up. The pain in his fingers had reached an excruciating level and then they'd gone numb. He looked at his fingertips. They weren't bleeding but they'd been bruised a deep purple.

He supposed he could have stretched the story another ten thousand words to put it over 50K and make it officially a novel, but that would be padding. Gilding the lily, as it were. Novella was the perfect length for this story.

Now, to get it to a publisher.

Frankie needed a shave and—he sniffed an armpit—a bath too, but most of all he needed to get this story back to his world.

After maybe half a minute, the cab stopped with a lurch and the door parted. Frankie stood and stared. No, not hell. But maybe a passage to hell?

Or a passage to somewhere else?

A rough-hewn, squarish tunnel, maybe eight feet on a side, carved through dark stone, stretched ahead of him, curving off to the left. Smokeless flames flickered in sconces spaced along the walls.

Okay, first question: Who lit the sconces? And second, what were the flames feeding on?

What did it matter? In sharp contrast to the blah, semi-modern, characterless buildings on the surface, this tunnel looked ancient. And that gave Frankie hope. Because it might just lead somewhere else.

Was it unreasonable to hope it led back to Manhattan–*his* Manhattan? Most certainly. Did he have a better route to follow? No.

With the manuscript of the Great American Novella clutched to his chest, P. Frank Winslow started walking.

Ernst

"Winslow never came back," Belgiovene said, slouching in the chair opposite Ernst's desk. "It's like he vanished from the face of the Earth. But don't ask me to keep waiting for him. I spent the better part of a day and a half sitting in his crummy apartment with nothing to do. Damn near went crazy."

P. Frank Winslow's laptop lay on Ernst's desk. He drummed his fingers on its closed cover. Belgiovene had stated it was the only computer in the apartment. That didn't mean Winslow hadn't backed up his writing to a storage service like Dropbox, but no matter. He hadn't called Belgiovene to his office to inquire about Winslow. The hack had been demoted to a secondary concern. Ernst had a much more delicate assignment for the killer.

"Let's put P. Frank Winslow aside for the time being. We have a more pressing concern."

"Oh?" His ennui was palpable.

"The Council has designated our loremaster a Threatening Presence."

Belgiovene jerked upright in his chair.

Now he shows some life, Ernst thought.

"What? Slootjes a TP? That's crazy."

"I was as surprised as you, but he's been denigrating the Council and the Order itself, and at noon he plans to spread his vitriol to the entire membership."

The big man frowned. "What's vitriol?"

"A fancy word for 'poison.'" Not entirely accurate, but better than trying to explain sulfuric acid to this man.

"Today? Of all days he's chosen *today* to dump on the Order?"

"I tried to talk him out of it but he's determined."

He'd reasoned with the loremaster for half an hour but Slootjes might as well have been stone deaf for all the effect Ernst's arguments had. When he'd informed him of the Council's Threatening Presence designation, Slootjes pulled a pistol and ordered Ernst from the archives, saying he'd defend himself against whoever tried to stop his message.

Ernst fixed Belgiovene with a pointed stare. "So I'm afraid it's up to you to–"

"Take him out? Me?" Belgiovene leaped from the chair. "No way. I don't whack a brother. That's a line I will not cross. Find somebody else."

And with that he strode from the office.

Ernst watched him go, then sighed.

I guess that leaves me.

He'd work himself up to it. On today of all days, the beginning of what he had worked all his life to bring about, he was being forced to eliminate a brother of the Order. He could almost hate Slootjes for putting him in this position.

He nursed the negative feelings, certain that the more he thought about it, the easier it would become.

Barbara

My mind still reeled from all that Ellie had just told me. We'd strolled the Coney Island boardwalk-down past the Parachute Jump and then back-looking like any normal mother and daughter out to breathe the salty air. But as we walked she'd filled my head with tales that were anything but normal.

She spoke of vast, unimaginably huge forces that spanned the multiverse. So vast and so few in number that they needed no names. Lesser beings with their need to classify and codify had concocted tongue-twisting designations, but the entities answered to no one, not even each other. They searched out worlds populated with sentient and sapient beings where they could toy with the inhabitants. Competition for these worlds put certain entities in conflict as one would try to usurp control of a world controlled by another.

Earth was one of those worlds in contention, and the histories of its civilizations had been warped and woofed by the influences and subtle intrusions of these entities.

"Our little corner of reality is about to change hands," she said. "The people who support the new landlord are delighted that the Change has begun. Those who support the departing landlord are terrified."

"But where are you in all this?" I said. "You're just a girl from the Midwest. Why you?"

"I was a girl from the Midwest who could hear the signals and was bathed in the Prime Frequency. Depending on one's perspective, I was the right girl in the right place at the right time, or wrong girl in the wrong place at the worst time."

"So if you hadn't been standing in that spot in the Sheep Meadow at that moment, none of this would have happened?"

"Correct."

I felt suddenly weak and dropped onto a nearby bench.

"So it's my fault?"

"Don't be ridiculous. I was determined to find the origin of that awful sound I'd heard."

"But I could have stopped you, or at last made you put it off till the next day...or delayed you even an hour."

"I didn't know it would sound again, or what would happen if it did. And you certainly couldn't know. So guilt is not an option here."

"But it's ruined your life."

Her expression remained impassive. "It changed the life I had. Now I have a new life."

Anger flashed through me. Whatever she'd wanted for herself in the future, whatever plans and dreams she might have had were all gone now, ripped from her. And she didn't seem to care.

"How can you be so...so...so *accepting*?"

She stared at me with those non-Ellie eyes. "What makes you think I have a choice, Mother? What's done is done. I can't change it and neither can you. I have a task to complete and then I am free."

My heart leaped. "Free? You'll be back to normal?"

"I will be free to do whatever I wish, but...normal? This is my new normal, Mother." She held out a hand to help me to my feet. "Come. We are due back in Manhattan."

"Due?"

"No one there knows I'm coming, but I'm needed."

We retraced our steps to the elevated D train and rode it to the Grand Street stop where we walked a block or two to Allen Street. From there we passed through an area full of Asians that I assumed was part of the city's Chinatown.

Eventually we turned down a side street lined with red-brick-fronted former tenements. Ellie stopped before a massive, ancient-looking three-story building of stone block that could have been a bank or a fortress. Its windows were deeply recessed within solid granite walls. Atop a set of wide granite steps, an intricate seal was suspended above a heavy inlaid door.

"What is this place?" I said.

"A lodge of the Ancient Septimus Fraternal Order. I'm needed inside. There's something I must do."

"Please don't tell me all these horrors have happened to you just so you could show up here and *do* something!"

She shrugged. "It's possible. Maybe I was pushed toward the Sheep Meadow so the signal would prepare me for this. Or...maybe I brought this on all by myself and am being sent here simply because I happen to be handy."

I wanted to scream. I couldn't bear the thought of my Ellie being used...a *tool*.

She started up the steps and I went to follow but she turned and stopped me. "I must do this alone. You don't need to see this. You've had to see too much already. Wait at that coffee shop we passed on the corner. Have a nice cappuccino and I'll join you when I'm finished."

"But—"

"They don't allow women, Mother."

"But you're—"

"They'll make an exception for me."

So saying, she turned and ascended the steps. I watched the heavy door close behind her, but I stood fast.

Have a nice cappuccino? I don't think so. That was my daughter in there. Alone.

I wasn't going anywhere.

Ernst

"Excuse me, Mister Drexler," said the acolyte from the reception desk. "There's a young woman here to see you. A teenager, actually."

Ernst broke from his reverie. He'd been working on a plan for Slootjes's elimination–the manner of his death, the disposal of his remains–but getting nowhere. And time was running out.

"A teenager? Asking for me?"

"She didn't ask for you by name. She asked to see the man in charge and, well…she said you had need of her services before noon."

Who was this? Some teenage hooker?

He was about to tell the acolyte to send her away when the phrase *before noon* struck a chord.

"She said 'before noon'? You're sure?"

"Positive."

Slootjes was planning to send out his email blast at noon. Could this be related?

What was the harm? The Change had begun. Anything could happen. He'd take a chance.

"Send her in."

A few seconds later the acolyte admitted a dark-haired teenage girl, rather pretty. But something odd about her–far beyond the oddity of the ratty old blanket she'd tied around her neck to wear like a cape.

Ernst stood and extended his hand. "Good morning, Miss…?"

"Ellie. Just call me Ellie."

As she took his hand Ernst felt a mild shock race up his arm as giant spindly spider legs sprang out behind her, framing her. He managed to repress a gasp and maintain a stolid front. He'd seen his share of strange things during his years in the Order. This was simply another.

When he broke contact, the legs faded from view. And abruptly the reason for her presence became clear.

"Well, Ellie, I was going to ask what service you thought you could render, but I think I know what it might be."

"I was guided here to solve your problem."

"Guided by whom?"

"The same who delayed the sunrise."

"And why would one capable of such a feat stoop to take part in this mundane matter?"

"I am not privy to that."

Privy...not exactly a typical component of the modern teenage argot. But then, this Ellie obviously was not a typical teen.

"Although," she added, "I might venture that the answer is simply: Because it can."

"But how will you.. ?"

"I am equipped."

Remembering his glimpse of those giant spindly legs, he nodded. "I'm sure you are."

"Where is the problem?"

"Right this way."

He led her down the dank stairwell to the archives where he knocked on the door. After a pause, Slootjes spoke from the other side.

"Who is it? Is that you, Drexler?"

Without prompting, the girl answered, "No, sir, it's me, Ellie."

"I don't know an Ellie. Go away!"

"Please, sir. I have something for you—something very important."

Another pause, and then the sound of someone working the lock. Ernst backed into the shadows where he would not be seen.

The door swung inward a sliver for a moment, enough for a one-eyed peek, then opened the rest of the way. Slootjes appeared, pistol in hand, but he held it down at his side. He looked even more haggard and wild-eyed than when Ernst had spoken to him earlier.

"Who are you and how did you get down here?"

"I'll only be a moment," the girl said as she deftly slipped past him.

"You cannot come in here!"

"Just one minute," Ernst heard her say as the door swung shut.

A momentary silence was followed by muffled shouts, a cry of terror, and then two gunshots. Ernst started forward, but then held back. Did he really want to see? He remembered the eight legs springing from her back and decided he didn't.

Frantic fingers fumbled with the inner handle, and then the door was yanked inward to reveal...

Loremaster Slootjes stood framed in the doorway, eyes wide, mouth agape, but his sockets were filled with black wriggling things, their legs raking his eyelids. They filled his mouth as well. His throat worked but only faint, strangled sounds emerged. He swayed, clutched frantically at the door frame, then fell back into the room as the door slammed shut again.

Ernst leaned back against the wall and closed his eyes. He hadn't known what to expect, but he hadn't been prepared for that.

The archives room quieted after a while, then the door opened and the girl, Ellie, stepped out.

"Problem solved," she said, speaking as if she had just adjusted a crooked curtain.

She passed Ernst and ascended the steps.

"The gunshots?"

"The shots went into the floor," she said without looking back. "No harm done."

Ernst started to follow her, then stepped back to the archives door for a look-out of curiosity, certainly, but also to assess how much of a cleanup would be required. He had expected blood but saw not a drop. His attention was drawn to the shape on the floor.

At first he wasn't sure what he was looking at, then noticed with a start that the disarrayed heap of clothing contained skin and had a human face-Slootjes's-though with hollow eye sockets and an empty, gaping mouth devoid of teeth and tongue. It resembled a human skin suit filled with a jumble of disconnected bones. Ernst had never seen anything like it and had no desire to see its like again.

When he reached the main floor the girl was nowhere in sight. From the front door he spotted her walking down the steps toward an older woman who could have been her mother. They linked arms and walked back up toward Allen Street.

Barbara

"What did you do in there?" I asked as we retraced our earlier path.

I felt, as her mother, I should know what my teenage daughter was doing in a strange building in Manhattan's Lower East Side.

"Nothing important. What is important is that now I'm released. No obligations. We can go where we want."

Could we? Really?

I nodded toward her back where those horrid little things clustered. "What about...you know?"

"They're content to be with me."

I experienced a strange, floating sensation, a feeling of unreality. Was this surreality our new everyday reality, Ellie and I? I surrendered to it. At least we were together.

"Where do you want to go?"

"I want to go see Mister Hill."

"Who's Mister Hill?"

"The man who carried me from the park last December when the Sheep Meadow signal triggered my...changes."

That awful, horrible day.

"I'll never forget," I said. "I remember his first name was Teel–no, Tier. But we have no idea where to find him."

"I do."

"Of course you do," I muttered.

She laughed. For the first time since Christmas week my Ellie laughed. And it sounded real and...and wonderful.

We returned to the Grand Street station and took the D train to Columbus Circle at the southwest corner of Central Park.

I gestured toward the park. "Aren't you worried...?"

"No. The Sheep Meadow signal will sing its swan song tonight. I'm actually looking forward to it." She pointed up Central Park West. "Come. He's this way...in the Allard Building."

"He lives in the Allard?" I said.

The Allard had the status of the San Remo or the Dakota. He hadn't struck me as wealthy.

The walk turned out to be a short one. We stopped before the canopied entrance to an Art Deco apartment building. Its sixteen-story base narrowed to a graceful, streamlined ten-story tower, capped with a heavy-duty antenna from another age.

A liveried doorman with *Simón* on his nametag greeted us at the front door.

"We're here to see Mister Hill," Ellie said.

"Hardly anyone asks for him by that name."

Curious, I said, "What name do they use?"

"'Burbank.' Is he expecting you?"

"No," Ellie said, "but if you tell him the girl he saved from the Sheep Meadow is here, I'm sure he'll see us."

Giving Ellie a suitably puzzled look, Simón retreated to his kiosk and made a call. He returned a few moments later.

"He said to come right up. Take the center elevator and press *P* for the penthouse."

The penthouse at the Allard...despite the horrors of the day I wanted to see it. The woodwork in the lobby was stunning–graceful arrays of multicolored inlays and laminates and burled wood veneers. The penthouse had to be even more impressive.

TOWER in Art Deco letters marked the middle of three elevators. Ellie pressed the *P* button and we whisked to the top where we were greeted by a tall and wiry man I recognized instantly: the same ruddy skin, high cheekbones, and sharp nose. Definitely a Native American. The only change was the fatigue in his eyes.

"Mister Hill," I said extending my hand. "So good to see you again." His clasp was brief but firm. "And this is Ellie. Remember her?"

"Of course," he said in a deep voice, turning to her. "But do you remember me?"

"Yes and no," Ellie said. "I was in pretty bad shape. Thanks for getting me away from the signal."

He looked surprised. "So...you know it's a signal?"

"Yes. I've learned a lot since then. And so have you. You put out a report on them, I believe."

"I didn't originate it. Burbank did. I merely took over for him after he passed. But now I'm shutting it down. All the signals have synchronized to the same frequency, so there's nothing left to report."

He clapped his hands once. "Well, it was nice to see you, but I'm busy dismantling the electronics in the monitoring room, so–"

"I want to go below and see where the Prime Frequency originates."

He stared at Ellie in silence a moment. As did I. What was she talking about?

"You know about that?"

She nodded. "It's among the many things I've learned."

He offered a lopsided smile. "Have you heard the expression, 'You can't get there from here'?"

"Maybe others can't," she said in a matter-of-fact tone, "but I can."

He shook his head. "The passage is closed, I'm afraid."

"It will open for me."

Another long stare, then, "You know, for some strange reason, I believe it will."

"Can we go now?"

He shrugged. "Don't see why not. We'll have to take the freight elevator. Wait here while I get the keys."

He returned a minute later and the three of us rode the elevator back down to the lobby. He led us to a rear corner and was unlocking a door there when Simōn called out from the entrance.

"Mister Hill? This lady here is in a big rush to meet Burbank."

We turned to see a short Indian woman striding purposefully across the lobby.

Hari

Hari took a Lyft from Newark Airport straight to the Allard.

She felt content and calm. Good sex did that for her. And the sex had been very good. Donny proved to be a skilled and considerate lover, as anxious to please her as she was to be pleased. She hadn't felt this relaxed in a long, long time. Too long.

And as a bonus, for a while she'd been able to forget about the sun rising late.

Despite her cajoling and even the application of some of the *Kama Sutra* techniques she'd learned, she could not convince him to return to New York with her. He was planning something. He kept saying he didn't have a plan yet but she didn't buy that. For some reason he didn't want to tell her what it was. Which meant it was either foolish or dangerous or both.

But Hari had her own plan, which involved learning more about the signals. According to Donny, the last report from *burbank@theallard.com* said all the signals had synchronized their frequencies. A few hours after that, the sun rose late. Coincidence? Hari didn't think so. And as far as she could see, if anyone had info on the signals, this Burbank character was the man.

She hopped out of her Lyft and headed straight for the doorman.

"Somebody named Burbank live here?"

The doorman nodded. "He's busy right now. If you want to leave your–"

"I'm one of his subscribers." Well, Donny had been reading his emails–close enough. "I need to speak to him ay-sap. It's important. What can you do for me?"

He turned and called out to a tall man and two women in a far corner of the lobby. "Mister Hill? This lady here is in a big rush to meet Burbank."

The man had ruddy skin and strong features. She didn't get the "Mister Hill" bit, but the way the guy had turned said he had to be Burbank. She made a beeline for him.

"Hari Tate," she said, shaking his hand. "Spelled H-a-r-i." She guessed from his complexion and features he was Native American. "One of your subscribers. I've got some questions about the signals."

"I'm busy right now," he said. "If you want to wait–"

"Last night they all synchronized, and today the sun rose late. There's got to be a connection."

He shrugged. "There's certainly a correlation but I don't know if it's a cause-effect relationship."

The younger of the two women, a teenager with a weird ratty blanket tied around her neck, said, "Night is falling, the Change has begun."

Uh-oh...was she one of those Septimus types? She was just a kid.

"What happened to 'twilight has come...night will follow'?"

"That's passé. Twilight is done."

"I don't think I like the sound of that," Hari said. "Who are you?"

She introduced herself as Ellie and the older woman as her mother, Barbara.

"And you're Burbank?" Hari said.

"My Burbank days are over. I'll answer to Hill."

Ellie turned to him. "Maybe we should take her with us."

Hill shook his head. "I don't know..."

"Hari says she wants to learn about the signals. The Prime generator would be an excellent place to start."

"If we're talking about something that generates this Prime Frequency I've heard about, I'm in. Lead on."

Hill hesitated, then said. "Okay, but don't be surprised if our way is blocked."

He opened a door and Hari followed the three of them into what looked like a freight elevator. He inserted another key into one of two slots in the control panel and the car started down.

"What's down here?"

"The Allard has an underground garage but we're going below that, deep into the schist. You can't access the bottom stop without a key."

"What's the schist?" Barbara said.

"It's the bedrock of Manhattan Island," her daughter said. "It runs close to the surface here in Midtown."

Well, I just learned something, Hari thought. Smart kid.

But something very weird about her–a keep-your-distance brand of weird. The ratty blanket as cape, sure, weird as hell, but something much deeper. And on the subject of the blanket, did it just move, like with a breeze when there wasn't one?

Hari was going to have to keep an eye on her.

After a long slow descent, the elevator ground to a halt. Unexpectedly, the door behind them opened.

Hari tapped the one that had stayed closed. "Where does this one go?"

"Just a rather large storage area where Mister Allard locked away mementoes of his life."

"He must have a lot of mementoes."

A nod. "That he does. I've only taken a quick look, but he left all sorts of things in there, including an intact autogyro."

"An auto-*what*?"

"Autogyro—a two-seat precursor to the helicopter."

Figuring that had to be one helluva storage space, Hari followed Hill out the rear door onto a platform and–

"Holy shit!" Hari cried and pressed her back against the wall. "I mean, what the *fuck*?"

That kind of language was not her style, but the words jumped out on their own. She noticed Barbara close beside her, eyes closed, looking a little sick. She understood perfectly.

A stone stairway led down–not against the wall, where you'd normally expect it, where any sane person would place it, but curving through the middle of the emptiness. With no handrail. Just steps, four feet wide and going down forever. Not into darkness–at least they were spared that–but down and down. Flames flickered in sconces all up and down the circular wall, lighting the stairway and all the empty space around it.

"Sorry," Hill said. "I should have warned you."

"Ya think?" Hari said.

Despite his rugged good looks, this Burbank or Hill or whatever he was calling himself was getting on her nerves.

Barbara still had her eyes closed. "W-we have to go down there?"

"I'm afraid so," Hill said. "I didn't realize you were acrophobic."

Hari forced herself to push off from the wall and take a few steps closer to the edge.

"I'm not. I don't exactly go looking for high places, but I'm not terrified of them."

"Same here," Hill said. "Even though my father and grandfather were skywalkers, I–"

Ellie said, "Like in *Star Wars*?"

"No, like in high-steel workers. Like many Mohawks, they had no fear of heights. I didn't inherit that." He waved an arm above. "My grandfather helped build the Allard and hinted that it held secrets in its foundation. I'd always assumed he meant gangsters from the Roaring Twenties had found their final resting place in the concrete, but I wasn't even close."

"Who clued you to this?" Hari said.

"The original Burbank occupied the penthouse from its beginning in 1931 to just last December."

Hari did a quick count. "From 1931? He must have been–"

Hill was nodding. "Yes, he died at a very ripe old age. He knew almost everything about the building and left lots of notes. I found a section of blueprint with these keys in his papers."

"We're wasting time," Ellie said, hands on hips, foot tapping. "Mother, maybe you'll feel better waiting upstairs in the lobby?"

"No!" Barbara said. She had her eyes open now but still looked a little green around the gills. "I'm...I'm coming with you."

"Don't put yourself through that," Hari said. "I'll watch out for her."

"But who'll watch out for you?" Barbara muttered. Before Hari could ask what she meant, Barbara added, "You all go ahead. I'll be fine right here."

"Sorry, Mother," Ellie said and started down with the nonchalance of someone descending steps a dozen times wider.

Hill followed but at a slower pace.

"I've been down these a number of times," he said. "The trick is to keep your head down and your eyes fixed on the next step."

Hari stopped on the lip of the first step and looked down and around.

"Who dug this?"

"Don't know," Hill said, "but Burbank's papers say it was already here when they dug the Allard's foundation. The owner, the original Mister Allard, would only allow natives of an obscure South

American tribe to work on the section of the foundation directly above this."

"How old is it?"

"Burbank didn't know."

"Okay, one more question then I'll shut up: all these flames burning in the wall...who refills the sconces?"

"No one," Hill said. "They never seem to run out."

Twenty-four hours ago Hari would have called *bullshit*. But after spending the night on another planet, she accepted that he was telling the truth.

She started down, using his method of watching the next step, and it worked to block out all the empty air around her. She'd almost caught up to Hill by the time he reached the bottom where an obviously impatient Ellie waited before a big, pointed-arch door of riveted steel set in the wall.

Hill flipped through his crowded keyring and selected the largest one.

"You have a key for every room in the place?"

He shook his head. "No idea what all these are for. Luckily they're labeled." He stuck the big key in the lock but didn't turn it. "Don't get your hopes up, anybody. Every time I've opened this door I've run into a wall."

When he turned the key, a latch went *thunk* deep within. He grasped the iron ring that served as a handle and swung it out to reveal...a stone wall.

"You weren't kidding, were you," Hari said.

"Close it again," Ellie said, "then let me open it."

Hill gave her a look. "You really think...?"

Hari looked at the solid wall of stone, the very bedrock of Manhattan, impenetrable. And yet...this weird kid had this air about her and, what the hell, anything and everything seemed possible today.

How had that mantra ended? *It will begin in the heavens and end in the Earth, but before that, the rules will be broken.*"

Well, the sun had been late climbing into the heavens, and here they were, deep in the Earth...and all sorts of rules had been broken back on Norum Hill...

"Give her a shot," Hari said. "What've we got to lose?"

Hill pushed the door shut and stood back. As Ellie reached for the ring, Barbara cried out behind them.

"Wait for me!"

The three of them turned to find her crawling backward down the steps on her hands and toes.

Barbara

I don't know how I did it, but I couldn't let my baby go off with strangers to see the infernal machine that destroyed her life. I found a way to bottle my terror and crawl down those awful stairs.

As I reached the bottom I stood and brushed myself off. I found Ellie and the other two staring at me.

"What?" I said, unable to think of anything else.

The Indian woman smiled and applauded softly while Ellie and Tier Hill showed little reaction.

"Ready?" Ellie said.

Without waiting for a response, she grabbed the ring in the door and pulled.

And with that the spider legs sprang from her back, poking through Blanky without disturbing it or the myriad black crawly things that hid beneath it. Hill recoiled and Hari sprang back, nearly tripping as she cried out.

"Holy fucking hell!" She backed almost to the steps. "What? *What?*"

I had seen those legs before but still wasn't used to them. I'd *never* get used to them.

The door swung outward, but this time no wall of stone blocked the way. Instead it opened onto a wide, dark hallway lit by flaming sconces similar to the stairwell.

Hill leaped forward and peered through, saying, "How's this possible?"

"Told you I could open it," Ellie said with a smirk. "You need to believe me next time." As she spoke her spider legs retracted. "Well, what are we waiting for?"

She stepped through the doorway. Hill took a step after her, then stopped. I couldn't blame him. Who'd want to be alone with her? That left it to me. I was about to fall in line when Hari grabbed my arm.

"I'm not crazy, am I? You saw that right?" I couldn't help the tears that sprang into my eyes. She spotted them and nodded. "Oh, yeah. You have. What...how...?"

I swallowed and pointed through the door. "If there *is* an explanation, I don't think it will be rational, but I've a feeling we're headed toward a big part of it right now."

"But where did those...legs come from? And where did they go?"

"She says they're tucked away elsewhere. Don't ask me what that means."

I stepped through the door and Hari followed close behind. Hill brought up the rear.

We entered a high-ceilinged hallway dimly lit by flames flickering in small, widely spaced sconces. It spanned maybe fifty feet wide. Darkness swallowed whatever lay above us, but I could see doors set in the walls. So many doors, all made of riveted steel like the one at the entrance.

Hari gestured to Hill's heavy key ring. "I guess we know what all those are for now. Where do the doors go?"

He shook his head. "No idea. I've never been in here. Burbank didn't mention them in his notes. I don't know if he ever got this far." He held out the keyring. "Want to open one and see?"

I almost laughed at Hari's shocked expression as she said, "Do I look stupid to you? Or crazy? If you notice, they all have locks. I will trust that they're locked for a good reason and leave them that way."

"They all seem to be labeled," I said, squinting at the weird symbols top center on each door. "But in what language?"

"Don't know," Hill said, flipping through his keys. "But I've got matching symbols here."

The walls and floor of the stairway chamber behind us had been smooth, almost polished. Less effort had been expended on this passage. Everything looked roughhewn, and I imagined the unseen ceiling to be no different. Perhaps even rougher since the floor was littered with chunks of fallen rock. I stepped carefully.

After walking perhaps a thousand feet we found our way blocked by a massive stone wall that had a Gibraltar feel to it. Part of the Manhattan bedrock, the schist. A steel door identical to the one that had admitted us was set in its base. Ellie, who'd reached it first, tugged on its ring but it wouldn't budge.

"I'm not sure which key," Hill said as we reached her.

"Try the same one as before," I said.

He did and the latch *thunk*ed. He pulled on the ring and the door swung open to reveal a large round chamber lit by the same flickering sconces that had illuminated our way since we'd stepped out of the elevator. A round, tapering structure squatted at the center, dominating the space.

Years ago I'd taken the girls on a tour of Hoover Dam that included the generator room where we'd stared in wonder at the huge turbines. This resembled one of those, only smaller. Its design had an Art Deco feel and looked...ceramic.

"This is it," Ellie said in a flat tone. "The Prime Frequency generator."

I stared at the thing and hated it.

I said, "This is what made you sick and burned you and put you in a coma? This is what changed you?"

She nodded. "As I said, wrong place, wrong time."

I looked up toward an arched ceiling. "Then that means we're directly under the center of the Sheep Meadow."

"Not necessarily," Ellie said. "Like my hidey hole, this chamber bends the rules of physics and geometry. It occupies its own space, one that's not always where it seems to be. When it emits its signal, it's under the Sheep Meadow. At other times, like now, it's...elsewhere."

Hill said, "I'm having a problem getting my head around that." He looked at Hari. "You?"

"Yesterday morning I'd have been right beside you on the confusion boat. But after where I spent last night, no, it's fine. Nooooo problem."

Which seemed an odd thing to say. But I couldn't let it distract me. I needed to know more about this thing.

"Who built it?" I said.

Hill shrugged. "Burbank told me the signals started in 1941, but according to his notes, the stairway and probably the tunnel were here when the Allard's foundation was dug."

I couldn't stay in the same space as this thing. I walked back out into the passage and burst into tears. I wanted—*needed*—someone to blame. This big, gleaming, soulless inanimate object wasn't filling the bill. I kicked one of the fist-sized stones littering the floor and sent it flying, wincing at the pain in my foot. I kicked another. More pain. I deserved it for letting Ellie lead us to the Sheep Meadow instead of insisting we go to the zoo as planned.

I'd let her go to where this contraption was lurking in the depths of the schist waiting for someone like her to come along.

Burning with sudden fury I picked up one of the rocks and charged back into the chamber. With a wordless cry of insensate rage I began hammering the side of the generator, screaming at it.

Hands pulled me away and pried the rock from my fingers as sympathetic voices tried to soothe me–the voices of Hari and Hill. Ellie stood silently by, watching with the eyes of a stranger, as impassive as the generator itself, which I hadn't even scratched.

I got a grip on myself and tried to explain.

"This...this thing," I said, pointing, "stole my daughter."

"I'm still here, Mother."

I stared at her. "Are you?"

Ellie didn't answer. Instead she turned and stared at the infernal machine, saying, "The generator will transmit its last signal tonight and then destroy itself."

"I wish it had done that a year ago."

"The time wasn't right then. Now it is. It has begun in the Heavens and it will end in the Earth."

"When tonight?" Hill said.

"After dark, for certain, but the exact time will be for someone else to decide." Ellie moved toward the door. "I've seen what I came to see. We can go now."

"Well, thanks for the permission," Hari muttered.

But she followed Ellie.

Hill moved to my side. "Not much point in staying. I made a circuit of the thing while you stepped out and found no writing or sign of controls or power source. Right now it's just a big dull inert device."

I nodded and led him out. We found Hari waiting for us in the passageway.

"I've still got a lot of questions about these signals," she said. "Like where do they come from?"

Hill waved an arm. "Out there."

"Oh, well, that clears up everything," she said with a sour expression. "Can we be just a smidgen more specific?"

I could have relayed what Ellie had told me about vast cosmic entities toying with us but I didn't understand it and wasn't sure I believed it myself, so how could I explain?

But even if I'd wanted to give it a try, I would have been interrupted by the banging sound that echoed through the passage.

"It's coming from over there," Hill said, pointing to one of the mysterious doors embedded in the right sidewall. He started moving that way.

Hari said, "Oh, you can't seriously be thinking of opening one of those."

I agreed with her, but Hill paid us no mind.

Placing an ear against one of the doors, he said, "There's someone in there. He's pleading to get out." He starting flipping through his key ring.

"*Think* about this!" Hari cried. "It might not even be human–just pretending!"

Which struck me as another odd thing to say. But only for a heartbeat. After what I'd seen in the past few days, it made perfect sense.

But what had *she* seen?

"I'm not leaving someone locked up down here," Hill said. He nodded toward the symbol on the door. "One of these keys has to match that."

He apparently found the key he sought, for he stuck it in the lock and turned. The door slammed open and a bedraggled man staggered out, holding a sheaf of papers clutched against his chest.

"People!" he cried. "Oh, thank god, *people!* I thought I'd never see another human being again!"

Hari

1

He said his name was Winslow–P. Frank Winslow–and he was a novelist. Hari had never heard of him, but she imagined a million writers were out there she'd never heard of.

She and the others led him to the stairwell and back up the insane stairway–Barbara crawled while they walked–then into the elevator and up to the lobby. All along the way he rattled on about a hole in the floor of his apartment and how it opened into a totally deserted city in another reality on another world and how he'd followed a seemingly endless serpentine path that eventually led him to the door Hill had opened.

Hari figured she could beat that story–she *wished* her alternate world had been deserted–and was only half listening until she heard him mention a familiar name.

"Wait-wait," she said, grabbing his sleeve. "What did you say?"

"I said I have to be careful not to run into Belgiovene once I'm back."

"Belgiovene?" Hadn't Donny mentioned that name? "You're sure that's his name?"

"Well, I overheard him call himself that when he was on a phone call. You know him?"

"Only heard the name. Could be someone totally other. Why would you want to avoid him?"

"He was sent to kill me."

Hari felt a chill. Donny said he was sure a guy named Belgiovene had killed his brother.

"How do you know he was sent and why would someone want to kill you?"

"The Septimus Order sent him–because I know too much."

Déjà vu body-slammed her: exactly the case with Donny's brother.

"Gotta go," she said and hurried toward the entrance without good-byes or an explanation. She had to check this out.

When she reached the door, Simōn said, "Can I get you a cab?"

"Sure. Thanks."

She stood under the canopy and dialed Donny's number while Simōn waved and whistled from the curb. The call went straight to voicemail so she left a message to call her ASAP. Then she took the cab down to the Flatiron District. She called Donny three more times along the way with the same result. Seemed like he'd turned off his phone.

Back in her office, she settled before her computer and found a strange icon blinking on her monitor: Donny's grinning face in a glowing circle. She laughed and clicked it. The screen flickered and a video of Donny began to play. He was standing by the damaged hood of their rented Tahoe. Initially she warmed at the sight of him, but then she noticed how stressed he looked.

"*Hey, Hari, I'm pretty sure this transmission will work. I'm beaming it straight to your hard drive. I hope you enjoyed our time together this morning as much as I did, and I hope you're looking forward to a replay as much as I am.*"

She was. As much as she knew it was foolish and couldn't go anywhere, she most definitely was.

"*Okay, that said, I wanted to prove to you that I can do more than sit and tap at a keyboard.*"

He waved to the woodsy scenery behind him.

"*I think you can recognize that area just a little ways back up the hill there.*"

She did: the cutoff from Norum Hill Road to the passage to that other place. What was he doing back there?

"*Remember I told you I had some unfinished business up here? Well, this is it. It's been a busy morning, lemme tell you. I contacted a few folks I've come to know on the dark web and arranged the purchase of a satchel bomb.*"

"Oh, crap!" Hari said aloud. "Don't!"

"*It's twenty pounds of C4 explosive. My little gift to those Septimus sonsabitches. Their trucks made another delivery. Another ten trailers and tankers, no doubt filled with more freeze-dried food and water. I watched them leave the mountain, so I'm here all alone.*"

He slammed a fist on the Tahoe's hood.

"*Damn them! They knew this was coming and didn't tell anyone.*"

Grabbed everything they could and socked it away for themselves. Big plans to profit from the shit storm. Remember how I told you someone needs to take them down? Well, that someone is me. I'm gonna see to it they went to all that trouble for nothing."

"Please be careful," she whispered.

She noticed the running time stamp in the upper right corner of the video. He'd recorded this almost an hour ago. That meant whatever he planned to do was already done.

Then why was his phone going straight to voicemail? And why hadn't he called her back?

Anxiety began a slow, tingling crawl through her gut. She didn't like this one bit.

"Like I said, the truckers have come and gone, the passage was open but now it's closed again. But I've got twenty pounds of C4 wedged into the mountain wall back there right where the passage opens. When I send the signal, a shitload of rock is gonna come down. Ain't nothin' or nobody gonna be traveling between worlds through there."

He leaned closer to the camera.

"It looks like I'm going to be able to get away with this, Hari. There were a couple of spots where things could've gone south–like taking delivery of the satchel bomb, for instance. You never know when a fed is going to be playing games with you. As insurance, I slipped a thumb drive into your bag this morning. It contains everything I've learned about Septimus and its operations. It's all moot now, but I'm just letting you know so you won't be puzzled when you find it."

He jerked a thumb over his shoulder.

"Showtime, babe."

Something awful was going to happen, she just knew it. She held her breath as he raised a cell phone and pressed a button.

Up the road behind him the side of the mountain exploded, causing the camera to shake and blur the image. Smoke billowed as shattered trees and rocks blasted into the air. It took a while for the debris to stop falling, but the smoke remained.

And so did Donny. She released her breath with a sob. He was unscathed. The young jerk was fine. He turned to the camera, grinning.

"I can't hear anything past the ringing in my ears, but let me say that you've just seen my personal 'Fuck you!' to the Ancient Septimus Fraternal Order. Next on my list: Belgiovene. If he thinks he got away with murdering my brother, he better think again. See you back in the city, Hari. Until then–"

A huge boulder dropped out of nowhere, crushing Donny along with the front of the Tahoe. The video went dead.

Hari screamed.

2

It took her hours and innumerable calls but Hari was finally able to track down someone who knew what had happened. The police in Williamstown, Mass, the town closest to Norum Hill, were totally closemouthed, but she found mention of the explosion on the website of the Berkshire *Eagle* in Pittsfield, and tracked down the reporter from there.

Her name was Alina Eastridge and she'd managed to get close to Norum Hill after the explosion, which had rattled windows for many miles around. She said the area was crawling with law enforcement types–local cops, FBI, Homeland Security, ATF. Early concern was that it might be a terrorist act, but now they were leaning toward a lone actor who had set off a tremendous explosion that apparently damaged only the mountainside. No indication why. The suspect wasn't available to explain because he and his vehicle were flattened by a secondary landslide.

Dead?

Yes, very dead.

The vehicle?

Rumor was saying an SUV, a Tahoe.

Hari sat in her office and stared for a long time. A steady stream of employees checked in, asking what was wrong and could they do anything. She waved them off. She didn't wail or cry or sob. Not her style. After her one scream of shock, she'd made her calls and learned the bad news. Donny was gone. She hadn't known him long enough to miss him, but still she mourned him in her own way: sitting in silence and staring at the blank windows of the building across the street.

And then she remembered what he'd said about dropping a thumb drive in her bag. Digging through the jumble within she found it and plugged it into her desktop. She scrolled through the contents until she came across contact information on a man known only as Belgiovene–email drops on the dark web, plus contact numbers in the real world.

Donny had done a good thing by blocking the Septimus Order's access to its hoard. Now she would do something for him.

She called Belgiovene's number.

Barbara

"Whatever you do," Ellie said, "stay off the Sheep Meadow."

The four of us—Ellie, Hill, Winslow, and I—stood back by the Central park volleyball courts at the eastern edge of the meadow where we faced the Allard. A near-full moon was rising behind us, shedding pale light on the grassy expanse and the buildings lined up across Central Park West.

We'd all spent the day together in Hill's penthouse apartment while he dismantled and repurposed the wide array of communications equipment clogging the main room. I found Winslow annoying in his insistence on turning any topic of conversation to himself, which might have been fine if he'd had an interesting life, but he hadn't. Most of his existence had been spent sitting alone in a room typing. His favorite subject seemed to be the supposedly wonderful novella he'd written about his stay in a parallel world, but that, again, was about himself. The only topic he seemed to like more was Hari. He kept asking about her—I sensed he'd developed an instant crush—but the three of us had met her only shortly before he had, so we couldn't add much. That didn't stop him from pestering us about her.

To get away from him I spent much of the afternoon watching the cable news channels, desperate for an explanation as to why the sun had risen late, but all I found were talking heads with impressive degrees who offered nothing but spews of empty speculation.

Ellie had immersed herself in Burbank's—the original Burbank's—hoard of antiquarian books. She stayed behind when the three of us went out to eat. Hill led us to a cozy bistro he frequented. I grabbed the check and insisted on paying since he was hosting us in his apartment. As the two of us argued about who would pay, Winslow ordered a coffee and Kahlua.

Back at the penthouse we anxiously watched the sun slide down the western sky. Sunset was scheduled for 8:06 but the orange globe was gone by 7:55. A fearful nausea rippled through me and I was afraid I'd lose the shrimp and capellini I'd had for dinner. We'd lost sixteen minutes of daylight today. I had a crawling certainty that tomorrow would be worse. Where would it end?

That was when Ellie had begun herding us down to Central Park to "see the show." Typically, she refused to say just what that show might be.

So now the four of us waited in silence, lost in our own thoughts. Well, make that three of us.

"The sun rose five minutes late this morning and set eleven minutes early tonight," Winslow said, restating the obvious. "That's the kind of stuff I wrote about in *Dark Apocalypse*, the novel Septimus didn't want me to publish."

"You mentioned that before," I said. "And you say they sent someone to kill you?"

He had to be mistaken. Ellie and I had been to the Septimus Lodge earlier. Although I'd stayed outside, and had no idea what had transpired within, I doubted they or anyone else would have reason to kill this inconsequential man.

"Yep," he said, hooking his thumbs in his belt and puffing up his chest. "I'm guessing I got just a *leeetle* too close to the truth about them."

Hill said, "I think I'm going to head back to the penthouse. I've got a good view from there."

"No, wait," Ellie said. "It won't be the same as being–"

"Hey!" Winslow said, pointing toward the Sheep Meadow. "Isn't that Hari?"

I squinted through the dimness and made out her form moving about in the center of the field.

"She shouldn't be out there," Ellie said. "Someone get her and bring her back here–now, before it's too late."

Too late for what? I wondered as Winslow took off running.

Yes, he did indeed have a crush on Hari.

Hari

Hari stopped dead center on the Sheep Meadow.

What the hell am I doing? she thought. I've gone certifiably nuts.

Earlier she'd come out to locate the spot in daylight, then she'd left a marker–a miniature American flag–stuck in the grass. Once night had fallen, she'd had trouble finding the little flag, but she'd managed. And now she claimed her spot.

For what? Revenge on a killer?

Belgiovene's initial reaction to her call had been shock. Only a very select few had his number. Hari had barreled on before he could hang up. It had taken a lot of cajoling and even threatening to convince him to meet her face to face. After all, the whole idea of operating from the dark net was the anonymity it afforded. But Donny's painstaking and laser-sharp research had provided her with enough info to convince him that his anonymity was a fiction where she was concerned. She had his phone number, she had his address, she knew of his Septimus connection, and even knew that he'd botched his last assignment against a certain writer.

That had been the clincher. No one was supposed to know about the Winslow hit and it convinced him that Hari had somehow opened a direct line into his life. She neglected to mention she'd heard it from the writer himself.

She convinced Belgiovene she wanted to hire him, but only on a face-to-face basis with payment in old-fashioned cold hard cash.

After much hemming and hawing and ranting and raving, he'd finally agreed, probably thinking no one could pull a fast one on him out here in the wide-open space of the Sheep Meadow. But he'd be standing directly over the Prime Frequency generator, with no idea of what lurked below and what it could do.

At least what Hari had been *told* it could do.

Hari had survived some horrifying experiences in the past twenty-four hours, yet none so unforgettable as giant spider legs springing from a young girl's back as she pulled on that subterranean door. What sort of madness had spawned that?

And yet the girl herself seemed unperturbed. A different story with her mother. Barbara had blamed the Prime Frequency for changing Ellie, had even attacked the generator.

But if the Prime Generator could do that to Ellie, what would it do to Belgiovene? Would it do *anything*?

Crazy.

But not as crazy as meeting a contract killer face to face in Central Park.

Knowing things could go south very suddenly tonight, she'd put her IT gal, Casey, in charge of Pokey, made it her responsibility to feed the crab until she got back. She hadn't told Casey where she was going, and hadn't said the real issue wasn't *when* Hari got back, but *if* she got back at all.

Meeting a killer. Really? This wasn't at all like her. She didn't get *involved*.

But Donny had pierced her defenses, slipped under her skin. His sense of right and wrong, his moral outrage at Septimus had reached her. The two of them had been marooned together on another planet-dear God, another fucking *planet*-and endured an attack by alien slime creatures. Even now, so soon after, those words running through her head sounded insanely absurd. And yet it had all happened. And they'd both survived it together.

Two people can't experience something like that and not form a bond.

And then this morning they'd made mad passionate love, or had mad hot sex-call it what you will, world, they'd pleasured the hell out of each other and had been planning a return engagement.

But then reality stepped in and changed all that. What was the saying? People make plans and God laughs. The Old Boy must be in hysterics right now.

The weight of it all-seeing Donny die before her eyes contributed no small measure to her madness, she was sure-coupled with the fact that Donny was unable to see this through himself, had spurred Hari to make this grand futile gesture of revenge against the man who'd killed Donny's brother.

And then the sun had set late, confirming her suspicions that a world of darkness and famine lay ahead. So what did she have to lose?

Hari wasn't a killer, couldn't imagine herself in a million years shooting or stabbing someone. But she'd seen what the Prime Frequency generator had done to Ellie. So if she couldn't kill the killer, she could at least mess him up beyond his wildest nightmares.

Of course, she had no idea this would even work. Maybe Ellie had been a special case. Maybe being in direct line with the Prime signal would do nothing to anyone else. But this was the best she could come up with on such short notice.

She did a slow turn. She had plenty of company in the Sheep Meadow. Scattered groups and solos, little more than shadow shapes, strolled or stood around. Some sat on the grass and smoked and drank, some made out. Belgiovene would be coming alone so she ignored the groups. She'd never seen him–Donny hadn't been able to find a photo–but his description was a slim man with a black mole on his chin. Not that the mole was much help since she wouldn't be able to see it until he was in her face.

She spotted a thin figure making purposeful strides straight for her. A sudden urge to forget all about this insanity and run for it nearly overwhelmed her, but she fought it and stood her ground.

He stopped before her. He had close-cropped black hair and the moon rising over the trees cast enough light to reveal the mole on his chin.

"You're standing in my spot," he said in a deep voice.

His words caught her off guard. "*Your* spot?"

"I'm supposed to meet a woman I do not know in the center of the Sheep Meadow tonight."

Hari found herself at a loss for words. She hadn't planned this out too well. How to keep him in this spot while she backed off a safe distance. And what was a safe distance?

"Are you that woman?" Belgiovene said. "Because if you–" He broke into a harsh laugh as he looked to his left. "You see everything in Central Park, especially after dark."

Hari followed his gaze to the west where a naked man stood with his back to them, looking up at the buildings along Central Park West.

Hari was about to comment when a voice started calling out her name behind her.

"Hari! Hari!"

She turned to see the writer guy, Winslow, trotting toward her. Of all people. Talk about bad timing. She was about to tell him to get the hell out of here when he skidded to a halt.

"You!" Winslow cried, staring past her.

"Is this a setup?" Belgiovene said.

And just then the ground started vibrating. That could only mean the signal was about to fire. She didn't want to be here when it did. She'd just taken her first running step when the earth gave way beneath her feet.

Suddenly *nothing* lay beneath Hari's feet. She twisted frantically as she began to fall along with Winslow and Belgiovene and the make-out couple and the drinkers and smokers–everyone except the naked man, now above her, floating over the emptiness.

She screamed as down she went, and down and down and down...

Barbara

"Oh, my God!" I cried. "Oh, my God! Oh, my God!"

Horror engulfed me as I clapped a hand over my mouth to seal off my broken-record cries.

Next to me, Tier Hill muttered, "What the–?" He tugged on our arms. "Get back! Back!"

"It's all right," Ellie said, as if something like this happened every day. "We're safe here."

The moonlight shone on a perfect circle of black emptiness where the ground had fallen away, vanishing from sight and taking Hari and Winslow and everyone else within its two-hundred-foot perimeter with it.

"A giant sinkhole?" I managed after catching my breath.

Hill shook his head. "Can't be. The park rests on solid schist. No place for the ground to sink to."

"Then how–?"

"*He* knows," Ellie said, pointing at the hole.

And there, in the empty space where the center of the Sheep Meadow had been, floated a naked man with outstretched arms that gave him the shape of a cross.

Floated!

Ellie added: "He did it."

"But who...?"

"That's the One. His time has come."

As I watched, he slowly sank into the black depths.

"Where's Hari?" I said, my throat tightening. I'd only just met her but I'd liked her forthrightness. "Is there any chance...? I mean, how deep is that hole?"

"No chance," Ellie said with a note of dreadful finality. "The hole has no bottom."

I didn't bother asking her how she knew, I simply trusted she did. But Hill snorted. "You can't really believe that!"

Ellie didn't respond, didn't seem to think it worth an argument.

The hole wasn't finished, it kept growing, more and more of the meadow crumbling into the abyss as people ran for their lives.

I heard a terrified cry and looked in time to see one of two ine-briated young men who had stepped to the edge for a better look tumble into the pit. More ground gave way, taking the second. A passerby almost lost his own life in a futile attempt to save the latter.

"Maybe we'd better back up," I said, eyeing the volleyball courts behind us.

The hole had expanded to three hundred feet and was still growing.

"It will stop soon," Ellie said.

And she was right. The diameter reached four hundred feet or so and stopped.

"Come to the edge," Ellie said.

I hesitated, then followed. Hill stayed a couple of feet behind me. Ellie stood on the very precipice. Hill and I halted a few paces back. I felt a breeze against my nape. Air was flowing down into the massive hole. I saw no sign of the floating man whom Ellie had called "the One."

"I don't get it," Hill said, indicating the emptiness stretching before us. "What's the point?"

Ellie stared into the depths as she spoke. "This is the first of many. Wherever a signal strikes the Earth, a hole like this will soon appear."

"But again," Hill said, "what's the point?"

"They will unleash the Change." With that, she turned to me. "This is where I leave you, Mother."

"What? No!"

"Neither of us can stay here, but for different reasons."

I knew I'd been in denial. I'd sensed this coming all along, but hadn't been able to face it. Still, I was stunned speechless.

"You have to gather up Bess and go home," she said. "First thing tomorrow you two must be out of town and on your way back to Missouri. There will be no safe place on Earth, but that storm shelter Dad built might give you a chance."

We'd all laughed at Ray when he dug that shelter and filled it with survival supplies.

I found my voice. "What are you saying? The shelter should be our home now?"

"That's exactly what I'm saying."

"But–"

"The daylight hours will shrink to nothing, Mother, and I won't be there to help you in the nightworld that's coming."

Nightworld...how could one word carry such menace?

"You're staying here?"

"No." She pointed into the abyss. "I'm going down there."

"You can't!" I said through a sob.

"There's no place for us here."

"Us?"

Just as I said that, those *things*, the little horrors she called her "kiddlies," ran down the back of her legs and scurried toward the hole where they crowded along the edge.

Hill recoiled, muttering, "Jesus!"

I couldn't help it, I began to cry, huge wracking sobs from the deepest part of me.

"Oh, Mom!" Ellie cried as she threw her arms around me, and right then I knew–I knew she was Ellie again, the real Ellie, my lost child. "Don't cry!"

I crushed her against me and cried harder.

"It's got to be this way," she whispered. "I have no choice. It's out of my hands."

And then she pushed away and her voice changed again. "Good-bye, Mother."

The spider legs sprang from her back then, and their tips poked the ground. They raised her off her human feet and walked her to the edge and over. The kiddlies followed.

I cried out and ran to the brink and might have fallen in had Hill not grabbed my arm. Reflected moonlight lit the upper reach of the smooth-walled shaft and I saw her walking surefootedly downward on her eight spindly legs.

I wanted to jump, truly, I did. And if she'd been my only child I would have done just that. Gladly. But I had Bess to think of.

Ellie quickly passed into the inky shadows and was lost from sight.

"I can't..." Hill began, then swallowed. "I can't believe that's the same girl I carried from the park back in December."

"She is and she isn't."

I needed to get away from this place, needed to find Bess and cling to her and convince her to come home where, according to Ellie, we might have a chance.

...I won't be there to help you in the nightworld that's coming...

Part of me screamed to stay, but I knew if I listened I might lose it and jump in after her.

I thrust out my hand. "Mister Hill...thank you for your hospitality today."

"Oh, that penthouse isn't really my place. I'm just living there for the time being, but I think I'll stay on awhile longer and keep an eye on things down here." He didn't release my hand right away. "I'm sorry about Ellie. I don't know what–"

I pulled my hand free. "Neither do I. Good bye, Mister Hill."

I was barely holding it together. Kind words of sympathy would reduce me to a blubbering puddle.

He nodded and we walked off in opposite directions, knowing we'd never see each other again, even if we both survived the coming Nightworld.

<the Secret History concludes in Nightworld>

THE SECRET HISTORY OF THE WORLD

The preponderance of my work deals with a history of the world that remains undiscovered, unexplored, and unknown to most of humanity. Some of this secret history has been revealed in the Adversary Cycle, some in the Repairman Jack novels, and bits and pieces in other, seemingly unconnected works. Taken together, even these millions of words barely scratch the surface of what has been going on behind the scenes, hidden from the workaday world. I've listed them below in chronological order. (NB: "Year Zero" is the end of civilization as we know it; "Year Zero Minus One" is the year preceding it, etc.)

Scenes from the Secret History is FREE on Smashwords

THE PAST
"Demonsong"* (prehistory)
"The Compendium of Srem" (1498)
"Wardenclyffe" (1903-1906)
"Aryans and Absinthe"* (1923-1924)
Black Wind (1926-1945)
The Keep (1941)
Reborn (February-March 1968)
"Dat-Tay-Vao"* (March 1968)
Jack: Secret Histories (1983)
Jack: Secret Circles (1983)
Jack: Secret Vengeance (1983)
"Faces"* (1988)
Cold City (1990)
Dark City (1991)
Fear City (1993)
"Fix" (2004) (with Joe Konrath and Ann Voss Peterson)

YEAR ZERO MINUS THREE
Sibs (February)
The Tomb (summer)
"The Barrens"* (ends in September)
"A Day in the Life"+ (October)
"The Long Way Home"+

Legacies (December)

YEAR ZERO MINUS TWO

"Interlude at Duane's"+ (April)
Conspiracies (April) (includes "Home Repairs"+)
All the Rage (May) (includes "The Last Rakosh"+)
Hosts (June)
The Haunted Air (August)
Gateways (September)
Crisscross (November)
Infernal (December)

YEAR ZERO MINUS ONE

Harbingers (January)
"Infernal Night" (with Heather Graham)
Bloodline (April)
The Fifth Harmonic (April)
Panacea (April)
The God Gene (May)
By the Sword (May)
Ground Zero (July)
The Touch (ends in August)
The Void Protocol (September)
The Peabody-Ozymandias Traveling Circus & Oddity Emporium
    (ends inSeptember)
"Tenants"*
The Last Christmas (December)

YEAR ZERO

"Pelts"*
Reprisal (ends in February)
Fatal Error (February) (includes "The Wringer"+)
The Dark at the End (March)
Signalz (May)
Nightworld (May)

* available in *Secret Stories*
+available in *Quick Fixes–Tales of Repairman Jack.*

ABOUT THE AUTHOR

F. PAUL WILSON is an award-winning, bestselling author of 60 books and nearly one hundred short stories spanning science fiction, horror, adventure, medical thrillers, and virtually everything between.

His novels *The Keep, The Tomb, Harbingers, By the Sword, The Dark at the End,* and *Nightworld* were *New York Times* Bestsellers. *The Tomb* received the 1984 Porgie Award from *The West Coast Review of Books. Wheels Within Wheels* won the first Prometheus Award, and *Sims* another; *Healer* and *An Enemy of the State* were elected to the Prometheus Hall of Fame. *Dydeetown World* was on the young adult recommended reading lists of the American Library Association and the New York Public Library, among others. His novella "Aftershock" won the Stoker Award. He was voted Grand Master by the World Horror Convention; he received the Lifetime Achievement Award from the Horror Writers of America, and the Thriller Lifetime Achievement Award from the editors of Romantic Times. He also received the prestigious San Diego ComiCon Inkpot Award and is listed in the 50th anniversary edition of *Who's Who in America.*

His short fiction has been collected in *Soft & Others, The Barrens & Others,* and *Aftershock & Others.* He has edited two anthologies: *Freak Show* and *Diagnosis: Terminal* plus (with Pierce Watters) the only complete collection of Henry Kuttner's Hogben stories, *The Hogben Chronicles.*

In 1983 Paramount rendered his novel *The Keep* into a visually striking but otherwise incomprehensible movie with screenplay and direction by Michael Mann.

The Tomb has spent 25 years in development hell at Beacon Films.

Dario Argento adapted his story "Pelts" for *Masters of Horror.*

Over nine million copies of his books are in print in the US and his work has been translated into twenty-four languages. He also has written for the stage, screen, comics, and interactive media. Paul resides at the Jersey Shore and can be found on the Web at www.repairmanjack.com

DISCOVER CROSSROAD PRESS

Visit the Crossroad site for information about all available products and its authors

Check out our blog

Subscribe to our Newsletter for information about new releases, promotions, and to receive a free eBook

Find and follow us on Facebook

We hope you enjoy this eBook and will seek out other books published by Crossroad Press. We strive to make our eBooks as free of errors as possible, but on occasion some make it into the final product. If you spot any problems, please contact us at crossroad@crossroadpress.com and notify us of what you found. We'll make the necessary corrections and republish the book. We'll also ensure you get the updated version of the eBook.

If you have a moment, the author would appreciate you taking the time to leave a review for this book at the retailer's site where you purchased it.

Thank you for your assistance and your support of the authors published by Crossroad Press.

CPSIA information can be obtained
at www.ICGtesting.com
Printed in the USA
LVHW091947120820
663006LV00006B/77/J